DAVID CAMERON'S
RETURN

DAVID CAMERON'S RETURN

GEORGE FREDERICK CLARKE

ILLUSTRATED BY
WILL NICKLESS

EDITED BY
MARY BERNARD

CHAPEL STREET EDITIONS
WOODSTOCK, NEW BRUNSWICK

Published by
Chapel Street Editions
150 Chapel Street
Woodstock, NB E7M 1H4

www.chapelstreeteditions.com

Library and Archives Canada Cataloguing in Publication

Clarke, George Frederick, 1883-1974
[Return to Acadia]
     David Cameron's return / George Frederick Clarke ; illustrated by Will Nickless ; edited by Mary Bernard.

Previously published under title: Return to Acadia.
Originally published: Fredericton: Brunswick Press, 1952.
ISBN 978-1-988299-15-0 (softcover)

     I. Nickless, Will, illustrator II. Bernard, Mary, 1941-, editor
III. Title. IV. Title: Return to Acadia

PS8505.L39R4 2018   jC813'.52   C2017-907898-4

Cover illustration by Will Nickless

The text is set in Adobe Caslon.

Book design by Brendan Helmuth

Cette nouvelle édition est dédiée à
GILLES GODIN
ET
ANNETTE SÉGUIN GODIN
grands amis de l'éditeur
grands amis également de toute la famille Clarke

CONTENTS

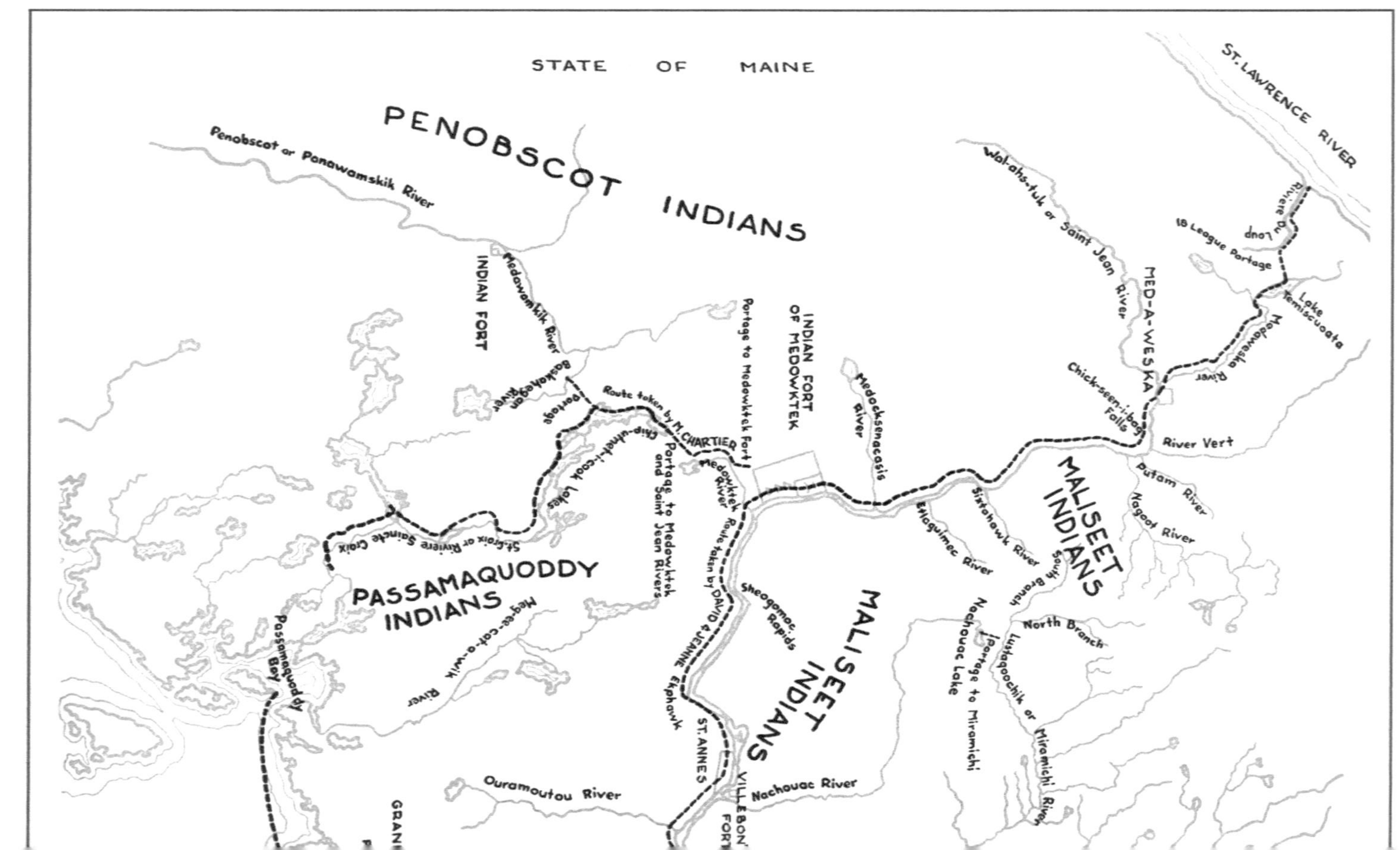
STATE   OF   MAINE
ST. LAWRENCE RIVER
PENOBSCOT INDIANS
Penobscot or Ponawamskik River
Wal-ahs-tuk or Saint Jean River
Riviere Du Loup
18 League Portage
Lake Temiscuoata
MED-A-WESKA
Medaweska River
Chick-seen-i-bag Falls
River Vert
Putam River
Nagaot River
INDIAN FORT
Medawamkik River
Baskahegan River
INDIAN FORT OF MEDOWKTEK
Portage to Medowktek Fort
Medocksenacasis River
MALISEET INDIANS
South Branch
North Branch
Lustaqoochik or Miramichi River
Portage to Miramichi
Nachouac Lake
Sixtahawk River
Etlagulmec River
Portage
Route taken by M. CHARTIER
Chip-utnet-i-cook Lakes
Medowktek River
Portage to Medowktek and Saint Jean Rivers
Route taken by DAVID & JEANNE
St. Croix or Riviere Sainte Croix
PASSAMAQUODDY INDIANS
Meg-ee-cat-a-wik River
Passamaquoddy Bay
Sheogomoc Rapids
Ekphawk
ST. ANNES
VILLEBON FORT
MALISEET INDIANS
Ouramoutou River
Nachouac River
GRAN

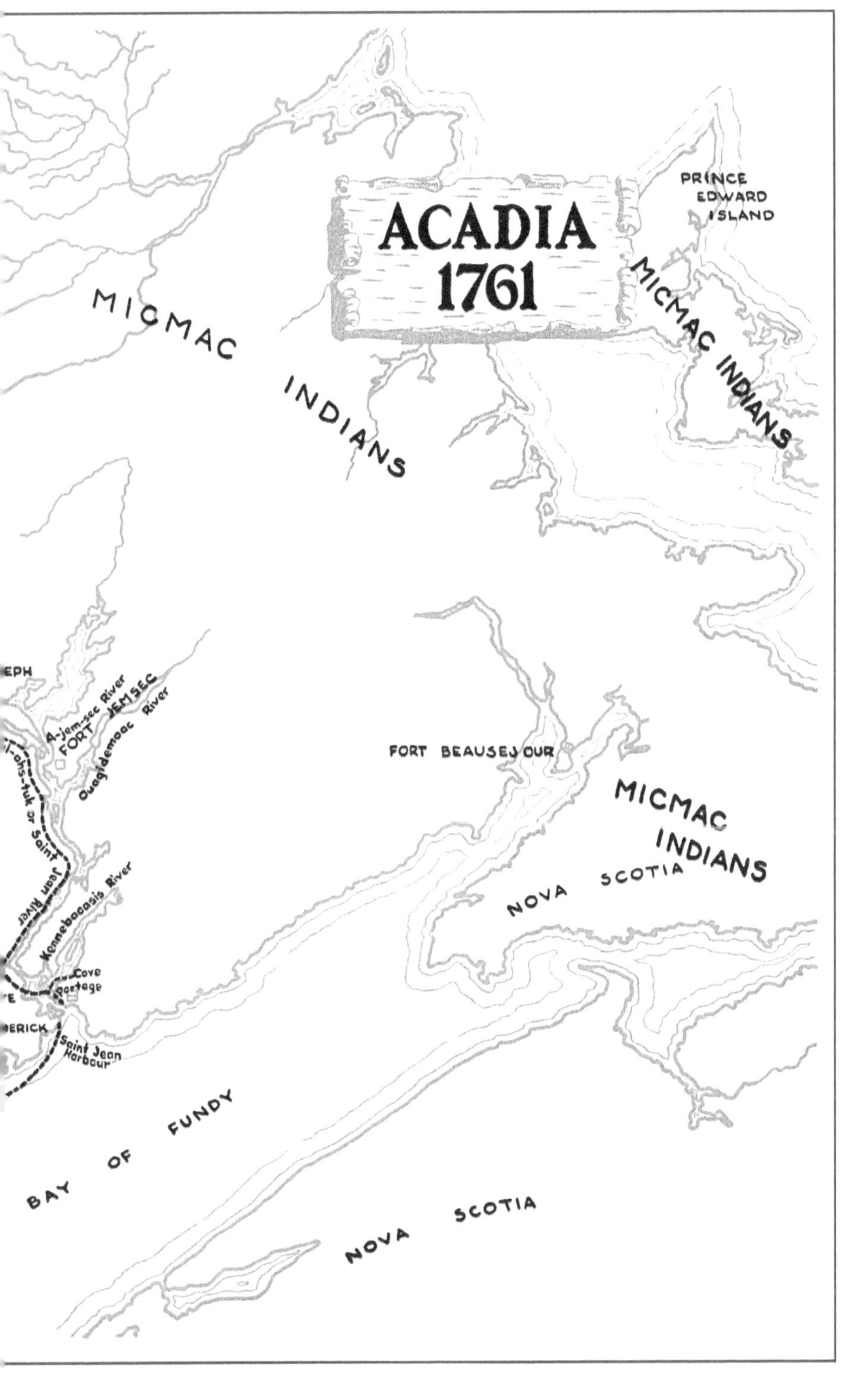

ACADIA
1761
PRINCE EDWARD ISLAND
MICMAC INDIANS
MICMAC INDIANS
MICMAC INDIANS
MICMAC INDIANS
EPH
A-jem-sec River
FORT JEMSEC
Ouagidemoac River
ohs-tuk or Saint
Jean River
Kennebacasis River
Cove Portage
ERICK
Saint Jean Harbour
FORT BEAUSEJOUR
NOVA SCOTIA
NOVA SCOTIA
BAY OF FUNDY
NOVA SCOTIA

EDITOR'S PREFACE

The title change

This book was first published in 1952, under the title *Return to Acadia*. The publishers and I find that title uninteresting and undescriptive, so we have retitled the book for this new edition. The title we have chosen isn't exactly catchy. It could have been called *David and Jeanne*, or *Love in the Wilderness*. But the title *David Cameron's Return* is as straightforward and foursquare as David himself, and it points up the link between this book and its predecessor, *David Cameron's Adventures*, the first of George Frederick Clarke's two historical novels.

David Cameron's Return is set in the mid-eighteenth century, in the part of Acadia that is now the province of New Brunswick. David is a leading character in both books. He was a boy in the first book; now he is a young man, returning to Acadia to keep a promise, and to find the woman he has loved ever since meeting her fourteen years ago, when she was a girl of twelve.

This new edition has an Afterword for readers who would like to learn more about the book's background.

I have provided a short glossary of place names and possibly unfamiliar words. They are marked with the symbols * or § the first time they appear, but not thereafter, so as to spare the reader a plague of symbols. The glossary also contains a table comparing leagues, miles and kilometres.

Mary Bernard
Cambridge
January 2018

i

1

As the *Sheila Grahme* sailed slowly up Saint John harbour that late August afternoon in the year of grace 1761, David Cameron stood on the forecastle deck and viewed with varied emotions the rugged shore line, with its forested hills that stretched for unknown leagues into the declining sun.

He had returned to Acadia, urged both by a promise made long since to a man he loved like a father—and by the desire to discover, if possible, the whereabouts of the girl he had briefly known as a child fourteen years ago.

Others have been lured to discover new lands by ambition, or to obtain wealth or spread religious beliefs. But I doubt whether Marco Polo set out on his remarkable journey to the kingdom of Kublai Khan with more romantic ardour than that which now animated the heart of David Cameron. Certainly David's pilgrimage seemed less likely to bear fruit than Marco Polo's. For fourteen years is a long time, and the effects of wars might well have removed the people he sought, far beyond discovery.

This place, known to the Indians of Acadia as Men-ah-quesk, was rich with storied past. Here had come Breton, Basque, and Norman fishermen a full century before Champlain and De Monts entered the harbour, raised the cross and the fleur-de-lys on its rocky shore, discovered the great river called Wul-ahs-tukw, and named it Saint John in honour of the saint whose name day it was.

Later had come Etienne la Tour and d'Aulnay Charnisay—rival lords of Acadia—each claiming the right, under royal charter, to the vast fur trade of the hinterland, which stretched in unbroken solitude northward to the borders of New France, and westward to the waters of the St. Croix, the Penobscot, and the Kennebec. And here had come Récollet fathers and Jesuit priests, to depart into the wilderness where, living in the bark wigwams of the aborigines, they had slowly learned their difficult language, and endeavoured to instil into their hearts the elements of the Christian faith.

Although more than a century and a half had passed since the French discovered the river, David knew that little effort had been made to colonize its fertile valley. Save for a few hamlets here and there, spread at wide intervals for thirty leagues, the vast area for the most part had been left to the Indians. And these, jealous of their ancient rights, and allied by religious ties to the French, had until recently proved an effective barrier to any encroachments by the English colonists of New England or Nova Scotia.

David could now see the English flag floating above the fort rebuilt by Colonel Monckton, two years since, then dismantled and abandoned after the fall of Beauséjour to the English colonial troops. He knew that Monckton, to make the conquest of Acadia complete, had taken a force of fifteen hundred men up the river to destroy the French settlements and send the few remaining inhabitants into exile with the Acadians who, three years before, had been torn from their homes and forcibly resettled in the American provinces.

Was it, then, a futile quest upon which he, David Cameron, had returned to Acadia? Did Tomah, head sagûm[§] of all the Indians on the river, still live? Had Jeanne Chartier, if living here at the time of Monckton's coming, met the fate of so many of her kindred? It was quite possible that she had long since gone to Quebec and married! Or was she still a maiden, and somewhere in hiding far up the Wul-ahs-tukw, on whose tributary, the Ah-jem-sec,[*] her father had established his seigniory and trading post?

His reverie was broken by the discharge of a cannon from the fort, and a round shot spumed up the water ahead of the bow of the *Sheila Grahme*—stern reminder to her captain to show his colours.

In a matter of seconds the Red Ensign was run up, and those of the crew not engaged in the management of the ship sent out a lusty cheer in greeting to those who manned the fort.

David now joined Captain Fortescue, master of the *Sheila Grahme*, named so in honour of the wife of his lifelong friend and partner in the shipping firm of Cameron and Grahme.

2

A little later David and Captain Fortescue were rowed to the beach, from whence they walked to the fort. Being met at the gate by a sentry, David made known their names, and asked to be taken to the commandant. The sentry called a soldier, who went into the fort. In a few minutes he returned and informed David that Colonel Arbuthnot would be pleased to receive them, and at once conducted them to his quarters.

The commandant was a tall, handsome Scot, long from the homeland. He eagerly asked for news, which David gladly imparted.

At length David said: "Colonel Arbuthnot, I can imagine that you are curious, and naturally so, to know what it is that brings me to this part of the world. With your permission, I shall first tell you a little about my boyhood life, which will, I hope, explain everything."

Colonel Arbuthnot gave him a quizzical look, and then said, "I shall consider it a privilege, Mr. Cameron."

"Thank you sir," said David, with a bow. And went on: "You are doubtless acquainted, sir, with the nefarious traffic in human lives that for more than a decade existed in the British Isles." He paused a moment. The colonel nodded, and David continued.

"My father was a notary of Aberdeen; our house in the Broad Gate. When I was twelve years of age my father died, and my stepmother had me kidnapped. I was put on board the *Bon Accord*— which already had in her hold more than three score boys destined for slavery to planters in Virginia. This was seventeen years ago, in March 1744. War had broken out between France and England. On the voyage over, we fell in with a French brig bound from Canada to France. Our captain overhauled[§] her, transferred her rich cargo of furs to the *Bon Accord*, and removed from her a Maliseet chief by name of Tomah, from Medowktek, which, as you doubtless know, is some fifty leagues[§] up this Saint John River, or, as the Indians call it, the Wul-ahs-tukw. He was on his way to France to visit his 'Father' the king.

"The chief and I became good friends. During the voyage to Virginia, he taught me many words of his language, and gave me the Indian name P'sazum. On reaching Virginia we were sold to the same planter, whose overseers treated the slaves in a most brutal manner.

"I shall try to be brief, Colonel Arbuthnot. We finally escaped together, and lived for about a year with a Delaware tribe. Then I was separated from him—captured by a couple of Mohawk runners carrying messages between the governor of Virginia and an official in Schenectady. But on the way I was again captured, this time by scouts—among them some Maliseets from this river—attached to Rigaud de Vaudreuil's army on its way to attack Fort Massachusetts.

"Following its capture, my Maliseet masters returned to their own village of Medowktek, and brought me with them. I was a slave there until, providentially, Chief Tomah returned, when I was set at liberty and treated with every kindness.

"Well, sir, in the autumn of 1747, learning that an English ship was at Casco Bay loading masts for the King's Navy, Tomah took me there. I was given passage to England; but before parting from the Chief, I promised him that some day in the future I would come back to Acadia and visit him. I have now returned. Can you tell me, sir, if a chief by that name yet lives at Medowktek?"

Colonel Arbuthnot took a deep breath: "Man, man, such a tale you have unfolded! Yes, the chief you speak of still holds sway on this river. A year ago, along with chiefs of the Passamaquoddy, Penobscot, and Kennebec tribes, he went with me to Halifax, and in the presence of the governor signed a treaty of peace.

"He is a bold, sturdy, independent warrior. But, although we have endeavoured to preserve good relations with his tribe, and have established a truck house[§] here for their advantage, they have given me considerable cause for uneasiness. Only a short time ago they turned back a party of New England surveyors who had gone thirty leagues up the river to St. Ann's,* a former Acadian settlement. Only a week ago, two members of the tribe came to the fort with furs. I asked them why the surveyors had been turned back; they answered haughtily that they owned the river, had always owned it, and would allow no English to settle at St. Ann's, or above it. Indeed, they were quite bold in their asseverations of sovereignty over the river." The Colonel paused a moment, then added, "But surely, Mr. Cameron, it is not your intention to proceed to Medowktek?"

"Yes, sir," answered David. "Such is my intention. That is the purpose for which I have come three thousand miles. Would you kindly tell me if the two Indians you spoke of have returned home?"

"They are yet here," replied the Colonel glumly.

"Good!" said David. "I had thought to go in one of my ship's smaller boats as far as St. Ann's, and there hire Indians to take me by canoe the rest of the way. But I much prefer to go all the distance by canoe. Do you, sir, happen to remember the names of these Indians?"

The Colonel nodded, and said soberly, "Yes, Mr. Cameron; one of them has the name Pemmyhawick; the other is Noël Sacobie." Then hastily, for David was about to speak. "Of course, Mr. Cameron, I have no authority to prevent your passage up the river, but I do question the wisdom of it. This Pemmyhawick is, I believe, an arrant rogue, and I much fear for your safety in his company. Must you go?"

"Certainly, sir," answered David. Then added, "I knew Pemmyhawick while I was at Medowktek. He was then one of the younger Indians. Sacobie is new to me. As for Pemmyhawick being a rogue," and David smiled, "I do not think he is as bad as your words would imply. Treat an Indian with trust and kindness and he will usually respond in like or, at least, that is how I found them."

"Ah, well, Mr. Cameron, have it your own way. But I shall feel relieved to see you safely back from your mad journey!"

"Not so mad," said David, with a smile. Then added, "And, sir, you are not to worry if I do not come for some weeks, In the meantime, my ship, loaded with goods for the Boston and New York trade, will depart thither, and when Captain Fortescue has disposed of them, he will return here and await my coming, be it soon or late."

Colonel Arbuthnot shook his head solemnly. "Like all Scots, you are as stubborn as…as…" He paused, and David said, smiling,

"Yes, that is what makes them such bonny fighters—if I may be allowed to praise us." He paused a moment, then added in a more serious voice, "Can you tell me, sir, if a Frenchman by name of Chartier, who once owned a seigniory at the mouth of the Ah-jem-sec, was living there at the time Colonel Monckton's troops went on their raid up the river?"

"That I do not know," answered Colonel Arbuthnot. "Certainly he was not there a year ago, when it was my unpleasant duty to lead a party of soldiers as far as Ah-jem-sec, in an attempt to round up some Acadians who had returned to the country. The fort and trading post, though still standing, had been deserted. I am sorry I can give you no further information." He paused a moment, then asked:

"You knew this Monsieur Chartier?"

"Slightly," answered David. "During my last few months at Medowktek, he came up the river with his young daughter on their way to Quebec, where he was to enter her in the convent school. At the time I mention, Monsieur Chartier was most kind to me. I have never forgotten it. And now, Colonel Arbuthnot," added David, "will you kindly inform me where Pemmyhawick and Sacobie are encamped?"

"Since I cannot dissuade you from going up the river, Mr. Cameron, I shall, of course, though reluctantly, send one of my men to ask the savages to come to the fort."

3

The following morning, David bade farewell to Captain Fortescue, and was then rowed to the east side of the harbour, where the two Indians awaited him with the canoe.

Having landed, the crew unloaded David's baggage, then sped back to the *Sheila Grahme*, whose captain was anxious to avail himself of tide and wind to take her out of the harbour.

It was Noël Sacobie who took the canoe by the middle cross bar, slowly and deftly raised it bottom-up above his head, and let it sink back until the paddles—which had been lashed to the inner sides—rested on his shoulders. Then he set off along the portage, used by the aborigines of Acadia for untold centuries, that runs over the high hill to the river and cove above the Falls. For these no canoe can navigate, even though the tides from the bay below rise so high that the current of the river is reversed twice each day between the great palisades of rock.

Pemmyhawick and David followed with what baggage they could carry, for some had to be left for a second trip. But David carried with him a gun he had had made for Tomah, his friend and head sagûm of the Maliseets.

When they had arrived at the cove, Sacobie put down the canoe, and while he and Pemmyhawick went back over the portage for the remainder of the baggage, David seated himself and awaited their return.

The scene that met his eyes was enchanting. The broad expanse of Grande Baye lay calm and unruffled between the encircling hills. On the surface of the water gulls moved slowly, like toys propelled by an unseen hand, or made short and seemingly aimless flights. Forest league on league, and above the horizon the sky filled with the purple haze of noon day: near or far no sight of habitation of man, or rising smoke above the trees from unseen cabin or wigwam!

All was primitive and peaceful, as though, thought David, it had been but yesterday that the Creator had paused from his labours, his task finished, and seen that it was good.

From Colonel Arbuthnot, David had learned some of the details of the devastation wrought by Monckton's soldiers: of hamlets burned; cattle destroyed or driven off; of men, women, and children sent into exile. Even most of the Indians of the lower river had retreated to their palisaded village at Ek-pa-hawk,* above the Acadian settlement of St. Ann's, thirty leagues from the river's mouth. St. Ann's had been fired during a night attack by Massachusetts Rangers, and some of the inhabitants massacred! The remainder had fled three leagues up the river to Ek-pa-hawk, safe for a time at least among the Indians.

And now, with the fall of Beauséjour, Louisburg, and Quebec, all hopes of French domination had finally died. And this noble river, this other gateway to Quebec, which Galissonnière, Montcalm, and Vaudreuil, had represented to their king as vitally necessary if they were to hold New France, had passed into alien hands!

What, David wondered, would be the fate of the few Acadian refugees above St. Ann's; and of those Indians who, despite the fact that their French allies had been defeated, still considered the river their own? He did not know. But he devoutly hoped that the victors would now be generous to both.

4

An hour later Pemmyhawick and Sacobie rejoined him. They ate, smoked their pipes, then loaded the canoe and began their upward journey.

It was all new country to David Cameron. For his previous knowledge of the river had been confined to its upper reaches, fifty miles above St. Ann's, known only to the Indians and a few French fur traders, or to couriers on their way to or from Quebec.

He noted that several large portions of the forest had been burned; the black trunks standing up gaunt and spectre-like. He asked Pemmyhawick what had occasioned the fire, and was told his people had burned the forest in revenge for the removal of their priest from the river.

They paddled until an hour before nightfall, when they landed and camped for the night beside a small brook. In the morning, after breakfast and the usual pipe of tobacco, they went on.

Towards midday they came abreast of a small river on their right, with a clearing and some buildings beside it. On being asked what name it had, Pemmyhawick answered that it was the Ah-jem-sec. Remembering that this place had included the seigniory once owned by Jeanne Chartier's father, David asked to be put on shore.

Having landed, they walked over the flat to the little knoll where stood the abandoned fort and trading post of Raoul Chartier. The fosse§ already had grown up with grass and small bushes. The fort was a palisaded affair, with four bastions connected by curtains.§ In the yard outside were the remains of a bark wigwam; in front of it a small circle of beach stones enclosing ashes and charred wood where some Indian had made his fire.

Leaping over the fosse, David pushed open the heavy gate of the palisade and entered the enclosure. It contained three log buildings. Two were midway of the fortress, leaving a wide space between them. The third building was at the rear, in the centre. From the roof protruded a broad stone chimney; and on either side of the open doorway were three small windows. The door had been wrenched from its hinges and lay on the ground.

He walked to the doorway and stepped inside: then stopped and gazed sadly on the scene of desolation before him. The floor was littered with broken stools and crockery. The plank table had been upended. On the mantel over the fireplace, in which lay a half-burned log, were two or three ends of wax candles. Everything of any value had either been removed by the owner, or carried away by Monckton's soldiers. David wondered why the raiders had not fired the fort, and concluded their commander had decided it might be made use of by English who would come later. There was a small room at either end, the doors sagging disconsolately. First he looked in that on his right. The straw mattress lay on the floor. He crossed the floor to the other bedroom. The bed had been turned upside down. A little table, one leg smashed, leaned drunkenly in a corner. A woman's worn shoe, with a tarnished buckle on it, lay in another corner. Quickly he went over and picked it up, wondering how it was that it had been overlooked by the soldiers. The buckle was hanging by a few threads. He removed it from the shoe; and now, looking at it more closely, he saw the letters M.F.J.C. cut into the face; on the opposite side was a small fleur-de-lys, and two or three symbols—possibly the hall-mark of the maker. Evidently the buckle was of silver. Could it have belonged to Jeanne Chartier? He was conscious that his hand holding the buckle was trembling. With a sigh he carefully put it into his pocket. He would polish it later on.

In this place she had been born and spent her early childhood. Here she had played; her only companions her parents—with perhaps a few Acadians, and Indian children from whom she had picked up their language. Possibly her only change, until she had gone to Quebec to enter the convent school, had been a visit now and then with her parents to some far removed neighbour. And yet, from his recollection of her during her brief stop at Medowktek, she had seemed a happy child.

As though it had all happened but yesterday, he remembered his first sight of her that Sabbath morning, seated beside her father in the Maliseet chapel at Medowktek: the pure beauty of her profile; the chestnut hair that curled from beneath the little velvet cap and fell to the white lace collar of her brown woollen bodice. The sun from the east window shone upon her, enhancing her loveliness, and he had been enchanted. In a sense he had been reborn, and he had felt that he would be contented to remain there for all time, and feast his eyes on her calm and spiritual beauty, that seemed more of heaven than of earth.

He turned, went out and rejoined Pemmyhawick and Sacobie. They were seated on the ground smoking.

And now the question that he had wanted to ask his paddlers so many times on the way up, but had desisted, sprang to his lips. Turning to Pemmyhawick, and trying to calm his voice, he said:

"Did you know Monsieur Chartier, the fur trader?"

"*Ah-ha*," was the quiet answer.

"When the English came up the river, did Monsieur live here?"

"*Ah-ha*, the white chief he stay at Ah-jem-sec."

Then David said, "And did his daughter live here at Ah-jem-sec?"

"*Ah ha*, P'oazum," answered Pemmyhawick, calling him by his Indian name, "the young white squaw she here with her father."

"Did Monsieur Chartier and his daughter go away before the English came?" asked David, and waited impatiently for the answer.

"*Ah-ha*," was the reply.

"And do you know where they went, Pemmyhawick?"

"*Ah-ha*; they go to Ek-pa-hawk. That is where we have *odanic* (a town)."

"Did they stay there, Pemmyhawick?"

"*Kadama* (no). When the English came to St. Ann's, and burned it, the white chief take the young squaw, and some French people, and go away up the river past the Great Falls—Chic-seen-i-beg."*

"One more question," said David. "Was Mademoiselle married?" And felt himself trembling as he awaited the slow, laconic answer:

"She did not have a man."

With a contented sigh David said, "*Wul-e-wun*, Pemmyhawick."
(Which in English is to say: Thank you, Pemmyhawick). Then he
added: "We will go now, friends."

As they walked back to the canoe, and entering it, proceeded up
the river, David felt happier than for many a long day. Tomah lived.
Jeanne Chartier had been here but two years since, had escaped
capture by the New Englanders, and with her father and others
had finally gone up the Wul-ahs-tukw beyond the Great Falls.
Moreover, at that time, she had not been wed. His hand reached
into his pocket to make sure the little shoe buckle was still there.

5

It was afternoon of the fourth day after leaving the mouth of the Saint John when David and his canoemen reached St. Ann's, called so by its former Acadian inhabitants in honour of their saint by that name.

David landed, climbed the bank, and gazed sadly at the charred and desolate remains of the log cabins, which but a short time since had known love and laughter, and beneficent sleep after the days' toil.

He would never forget Colonel Arbuthnot's relation of the midnight raid by Massachusetts Rangers; or that the Colonel had added: "War is war; but I do not believe in killing defenceless women and children."

Here had been a little chapel, whose bell, sent all the way from France, had rung out its mellow notes, and, awaking alien echoes in its wilderness home, had summoned alike the devout Acadians and their red brethren to holy worship of the one God.

David's eyes swept over the five or six hundred acres of cleared land, wrung by arduous toil from the forest, then back to the scene of desolation wrought by man that cold night in late January, 1759.

Such, he knew, had also been the fate of many hamlets of New England and of the Hudson River and its tributaries, during the border strife that had raged intermittently between French and English in America, with Indian allies on both sides, for the last hundred years.

Finally, with a sigh, he turned to his companions, thinking to resume the journey. But the Indians, who belong to a race deliberate in all things, remained seated on the bank. Then Pemmyhawick said: "We will have one smoke. You give us some of your tobacco, P'sazum?"

"*Ah-ha*," said David. Knowing that the Indian meant they would smoke one pipe-full of tobacco before going on, he took out his tobacco box and tendered it to him.

Both Pemmyhawick and Sacobie opened the little bag each carried about his neck by a string of rawhide, removed their pipes, and carefully filled them.

Although he was in a hurry to be off, David well knew that no amount of persuasion would induce them to depart before they had quite finished one smoke, so he filled and lighted his own pipe, and, restraining his impatience, sat down beside them, to let his eyes rest on the opposite shore, where three-score years before, at the mouth of the Nashwaak, the redoubtable Governor Villebon had built Fort St. Joseph, to guard the river for his master and ensure the continued loyalty of the Indians. There had gathered Kennebecs and Penobscots, Maliseets and Micmacs, to receive the presents annually sent by their "father" the king of France.

Hither had come New England troops pledged to capture the fort. But, although outnumbering the defenders four to one, they had been met with such discharges of cannon balls, and musketry from French and Indians, that they had ignominiously lifted the siege and fled down the river. Long since, brambles and alders had overgrown the spot where Villebon had harangued his tawny allies before sending them by river, lake, and portage against the New England settlers.

From that place Micmac, Maliseet, Penobscot, and Kennebec chiefs had been sent to France, whence they returned decked out with medals and fine clothes, and more impressed than ever with the might of their father the King, and his assurance of continued protection.

And now, high above the Nashwaak, an osprey leisurely and persistently circled, as though it were a messenger sent by the Fates to discover if puny man had decided again to challenge their decree and build anew.

David was dimly conscious that Pemmyhawick and Sacobie had finished their smoke. And now, as each restored his pipe to the little pursed bag, David tapped out the ash of his own, rose to his feet, and heard Sacobie say, "We will look at Tomah's gun now."

They had inspected it half a dozen times since leaving the fort. But concealing his annoyance, David again took it out of its case and put it in Sacobie's hands. Whereupon both he and Pemmyhawick examined it from butt to muzzle; ran their fingers over the letters David had instructed the gunsmith to cut into the brass plate inserted in the stock. They felt the lock and flint, looked at the pan, touched the brass-shod ramrod; then back to the lettering on the plate, the while talking between themselves in their low, musical tongue. Finally Pemmyhawick said, "What does it say, P'sazum?"

Although he wondered how much longer they would delay, David patiently read the words: "To Tomah, the Maliseet Chief, the friend and second father of Kuluwazu P'sazum."

Now the gun was restored to his hands, and Pemmyhawick said, "We will go now." And Sacobie nodded assent.

6

And so yet farther into the interior went the canoe, carrying David Cameron to his rendezvous with Sagûm Tomah, head chief of all the Maliseets on the river, where he hoped to learn the abiding place of her he had loved as a child.

This noble river had seen those Acadians who had escaped exile, either in canoes, or trudging along its shores, on their long journey to Quebec. Or it had seen them pause at some spot, remote—as they thought—from their enemies; rear their rude habitations out of the primeval wilderness; and start life anew.

And all the birds of the air, and the animals of the forest, especially *Mah-ti-gwess* (the rabbit), who knows all things, knew that these poor people had fled this way, even as all animate creatures flee from the devastating breath of forest fires.

And the salmon of the river, who are so wise that, having been hatched in a particular stream, they leave it after two years and go down to the sea; and during their sojourn there breast all the tides of the Atlantic, where they grow big, and then unerringly return to the place they were born, even to the far waters of the Na-goot*—even they knew of the passing of the Acadian canoes as they fled to fancied safety. With some of these Jeanne Chartier and her father had fled—above the great falls of Chic-seen-i-beg, Pemmyhawick had informed him. Whether they had gone on to Quebec the Scot did not know. If they had, he would go there, he told himself.

Now this resolve of his was singular, and required courage. For, although in his business and social dealings with men his approach was marked with great dignity and assurance, he was hesitant and shy in the presence of women.

They came to a series of islands, one of which was Ek-pa-hawk, the site of a Maliseet village, now surpassing in importance the old town of Medowktek, forty miles further on. But since David had firmly told his canoemen that he did not want to make a stop, they passed it, going along the right-hand shore of the mainland.

At this place the tidal flow from the Bay expends itself, and it is the beginning of the swift water. Pemmyhawick and Sacobie now discarded their paddles, and, each picking up his long, black-spruce setting pole, they stood upright in the canoe, one at the bow, the other at the stern. There was now no sound save the rippling of the water along the sides of the canoe, and the thud of the setting poles on the rocky bottom of the river, that, serpent-like, spread its vast length between the encircling shores where, from intervale to distant upland, the mighty forest, sentient with untranslatable mystery, clothed the land with splendour.

The Indians spoke only occasionally. Talk would come later, when they had made camp for the night. David was content to have it so. Words were banal in the presence of all this peace and beauty.

Occasionally a salmon leaped in some rapid; or again, from a placid pool, one would fling itself into the air, to fall backwards and shatter like breaking glass the river's face. Here and there a kingfisher dropped like a plummet into a still pool, miraculously emerged—sometimes a small fish in its beak—then shot like an arrow to shore to ease its hunger. They disturbed numerous flocks of ducks, which, now nearly full-grown, fled with haste in the wake of their wise parents.

7

They came in sight of Medowktek late the following afternoon. While yet some distance off, Pemmyhawick, who was in the bow, momentarily ceased poling, and, cupping his mouth with his two hands, sent out a loud whoop that reached the village; for David could see some of the inhabitants rush to the bank to gaze at the oncoming canoe.

From where he sat David could see the chapel, and the stockaded fort, with a double row of bark wigwams beside it. There he had spent months of slavery, had known ridicule and physical abuse, until finally Tomah had arrived and given him honoured freedom among his people.

It had been an important place during the French-English wars; for it guarded the famous Indian portage that led to Eel River and then, by a series of lakes and small streams connected by other portages, into New England. Hither had come Micmacs from as far distant as Gaspé and Cape Sable, and, joining with their Maliseet allies, had sped over the ancient route to ravage the English colonial hamlets and bring back prisoners and loot.

How long the Indians had occupied the valley of the Saint John, or from whence they had come, no man knew. David remembered Tomah's answer to his question; it was to the effect that Gluskap, the Maliseet tribal divinity, had brought his forefathers to the river long, long before the coming of the white man; and, seeing that it was beautiful, as also the lowlands and uplands, they had named it Wul-ahs-tukw.

The canoe was now close to shore in the little cove below the fort. Men, women, and children had rushed down to the sandy beach. Two squaws seized the bow of the canoe, drew it in, the while glaring fiercely at David.

He rose slowly to his feet, and, his eyes sweeping over the crowd, said in Maliseet: "*Ba-kwe-nox-e-wun, Ne-tup-uk?*" (How do you do, friends).

They spoke no word. All stared in amazement at this white stranger who greeted them so familiarly in their own language.

Now David stepped carefully out on the beach, Tomah's gun under one arm, and looking to the bank above he saw and recognized the tall, noble figure of the chief.

Gently forcing his way through the crowd, David climbed the path, and coming to the chief curiously regarding him, said: "Do you not know me, Sagûm Tomah?"

Slowly the chief shook his head. "*Kadama* (no), is it one of the English from the fort?" he said haughtily.

Then, with a smile, David removed his hat, showing his red hair, which years ago had aroused the wonder of Indians from Virginia to the river of the Maliseets in Acadia.

And now glad recognition gleamed in Tomah's dark eyes. "It is P'sazum—the little English!" he cried. For such they had called him in the old days.

"Yes, my father," said David, "I have returned as I gave you promise."

Then, with a quick step forward, Tomah took him by the hand and gave it a grip that made David's fingers tingle. And the Chief said in his soft tongue, "My son has come back. It is good. Tomah is made happy."

Now David put into his hands the gun he had had the gunsmith in Aberdeen make for him, with his name cut into the brass plate inserted in the stock. It was looked at and admired by each member of the tribe, men, women, and children; and each said it was *wul-e-na-gwit* (a beautiful gun).

Then, for David's baggage had been carried up from the canoe, he took out a long tartan as worn for ages past by his mother's clan, the Frasers, which he had brought for Tomah's squaw.

He was always to remember her face when he put the tartan into her hands, and she slowly unfolded it. Schooled to show little or no emotion, her plain face lighted up with unalloyed pleasure, so that it looked beautiful. Then, running her forefinger over the varied pattern, she looked up at him and said:

"*Wul-e-na-gwit Wul-e-wun, P'sazum.*" (Which is to say in English: It is beautiful. Thank you, P'sazum.)

Then he explained to her that the stripes of various colours, crossing at right angles in the plaid, made the particular design of his own mother's clan, and by it enemies, as well as friends, could distinguish them from others.

She nodded her head understandingly, and said, "*Ah-ha*, it is P'sazum's *tups-ko-d-gan*." (It is P'sazum's totem.)

Then Tomah, who with several of his warriors had been to Quebec, and fought in the Battle of the Plains, examined the tartan with great care. Finally, he turned to David, and said in French, "Les ecosses sauvages. Les petites jupes." Then he added in Maliseet, "They were wild men; they threw down their guns, pulled out big swords, run all the same as deer; chase French; chase Indians. Not stop for anything."

That was all. But David knew that his tartan had caused the Chief to remember that the Highlanders who had fought at Quebec had worn kilts and tartans with marking on them similar to those on the tartan he had brought Tomah's wife.

David remained that night with Tomah. And the chief confirmed what Pemmyhawick had told him about Monsieur Chartier and his daughter, with other Acadians, fleeing up the river beyond the falls of Chic-seen-i-beg. But Tomah was more explicit than David's canoemen: for he told him that they had settled at the mouth of the Medaweska River, which vents itself into the Saint John from a great lake called Tem-is-quoata, that is far to the northward.

At David's enquiry whether the daughter of Monsieur Chartier was married, Tomah made this answer: "*Kadama* (no), my son. She was not married when I saw them on my return from Quebec. Might be she is married now—Tomah does not know."

"Well then, said David, "I will go and find out. Will you take me to Medaweska, my father?"

"*Ah-ha*," answered the Chief. "Tomah goes where his son goes. When does my son leave?"

"To-morrow," replied David.

Before he slept that night he wrote a letter to Captain Fortescue in care of the commandant of the garrison at Fort Frederick. In it he told his captain that he had safely arrived at Medowktek and was presently going farther up the river, and for him not to worry should he not return to the fort for some weeks.

To this day, the Indians of Medowktek tell among themselves how P'sazum went up the river with their chief to Medaweska. But only Tomah, their great Sagûm, knew what happened there; and since he chose not to tell them, they asked not, it being against their nature to express curiosity about the private affairs of other people.

8

In the morning, after blankets and food had been put into
Tomah's canoe, David seated himself in the middle of a small seat
made of ash splints, the back of which rested against the centre
cross-bar. Then Tomah stepped lightly into the stern, and pushed
off towards Medaweska.

The Chief stood with his left foot slightly in advance of his
right, his tawny hands clasped about the handle of his long, black-
spruce setting pole. As he shoved the canoe resistlessly forward,
his hands shifted automatically, one above the other; his knees
bent, straightened, the muscles in his arms standing out with each
sustained effort. He was a oneness with each movement of his
canoe; as much a part of it as though he had been built into it when
its form was laid.

Most of the time he poled along the more shallow shore water,
where the current exerts less resistance to canoe travel; though
occasionally, as when there was a deep eddy, and no pole bottom, he
had recourse to his paddle. At other times when the current made
a sudden set to left or right over some gravelly or boulder-strewn
bar, he had of necessity to cross the river and take that side.

He navigated the swift rapids known as the Boiling Kettle, where
the water is black and deep, and cross currents form a dangerous
whirlpool in mid-stream, so that it is like an enormous cauldron
in which the river, whirling in a great oily circle, suddenly bulges
upward with a dull roar, to spread itself like white-hot metal against
the resurging waves. And having done this, the Indians say The
Kettle has once more boiled over.

With this part of the river David had been familiar. But now
the element of danger and excitement thrilled him anew. The years

at home had given him their share of activity. The ships he and Ian Grahme had built, or acquired by purchase, had carried him to most of the ports of the Old World. But although he had been thrilled by glittering mosques and stately cathedrals, and all the varied peoples in foreign cities, and at home in the British Isles, there had always been in his heart an ineradicable nostalgia for this land of Acadia—this enchanting land.

As a lad he had been conscious of its spell, and, now that he had returned, he was filled with renewed wonder and admiration. Gazing on the distant hills, he saw the lordly pines, like antique etchings, against a background of purple haze that stretched endlessly along the horizon, and merged, almost imperceptibly, in the blue above. In the foreground, were yellow and black birch, beech and spruce, fir and hemlock, with occasional clumps of maples that an early frost had already limned with a symphony of golds and reds; like a tapestry, he thought—like some rare and ancient tapestry of the exotic East. Here and there on the high bank were white birches, like pale tapers set between the more sombre and unimpassioned evergreens; along the shores clusters of red willow and hazel; the goldenrod and the ruby-coloured berries of the mountain ash.

And David marvelled that such beauty could exist throughout all the centuries, and be known only to wandering Indians plying their bark canoes along their ancient waterways. For he knew from his past life with them that they *were* conscious of it. And their word for all that is inanimate and beautiful is *Wul-e-na-gwit*, and to hear them say it is like listening to part of a poem—a singing poem.

The water purled from the sharp, upturned bow of the canoe; the gentle sway of the light craft, the thud of Tomah's setting pole on the rocky bottom of the river, brought back memories of fourteen years before that were painful as well as pleasant. In fancy he once again stood on the high bank near Medowktek Fort, his eyes fixed on the young daughter of Raoul Chartier, for whom he had caught trout the day before. He remembered the deliberate movements of the Indian in the stern as he thrust down his setting pole and the canoe gathered headway; the feeling of utter desolation that had swept over him; the sudden tears that had dimmed his eyes, as the canoe, and all it held, finally became a mere speck on the far bosom of the waters.

In that young Acadian girl's face and hazel eyes he had had a glimpse of loveliness that transcended all his boyish dreams, then was withdrawn, and he was left desolate. He remembered how he had gone to Tomah's wigwam, flung himself face down on the bear-skin rug, and wept heart-brokenly.

During the succeeding days his mind had been filled with thoughts of her, and, because he had come by the same route the year before, his fancy had followed each phase of her journey. He could see them arrive at Lake Temisquoata, the beginning of the portage on the left-hand shore, disembark, take the canoes out of the water, the Indians going before, their light craft over their heads; Jeanne and her father bringing up the rear. Almost could he hear the soft pad of their moccasined feet, see the sway of her lithe young body as she picked her way over the long portage to Rivière-du-Loup.

He had remembered how interminable the journey had seemed to *him*; his anxiety that possibly his Indian companions, Moxus and Arodowish, had missed the way.

Of course they would all rest quite frequently; for Jeanne was but a girl of twelve years, and the portage eighteen leagues long. They would stop and camp two nights, possibly three.

Finally, he had visioned her entering the convent school at Quebec with other French girls. But none so fair as she.

All these, and more too, had recurred to him times without number in the years following his return to his native land. Often he had wondered if she had finally wed. It must be so, for he felt that all men must love and desire her.

Now he was going to her. What reception he would meet with he did not know; but he was convinced that much of his future happiness in this world rested with the Acadian girl, who, on that far-off day at Medowktek, had fired his young heart with an adoration that had never lessened throughout the long years.

9

They came to the mouth of the Et-la-guim-ek;* which means in the Maliseet tongue "salmon spawning place", or, more literally, the actual act of spawning. In the ice-cold depths they could see hundreds of the fish, tail to tail, side to side. They floored the bottom of the pool, and, when they moved at the approach of the canoe, were like a cloud speeding beneath the surface of the water.

Tomah drew in to the beach and, holding the canoe, said to David, "You take the paddle, P'sazum. Tomah will spear a *pul-am* (salmon)."

It was fourteen years since David Cameron had handled a canoe; but as he took the paddle and steered the craft out into deeper water, he felt as if it had been only yesterday.

Tomah was standing up, spear in hand, peering into the bluish water. Suddenly, with a lightning like thrust, the jaws of the spear dove beneath the surface. The canoe quivered. The fish he had struck struggled a few moments within the confining jaws. With a low laugh Tomah lifted it into the canoe, and said to David, "*Mitz-o-wa-gun*, P'sazum. (Time for food, P'sazum.) We will go to shore."

They landed, made a fire. Tomah picked up the iron pot he had brought with him, half filled it with water and hung it over the blaze. Then he cleaned the salmon and cut off a generous portion for their immediate need.

David opened his pack and took out a little copper kettle, a box of salt, a cannister of China tea, and some lump sugar supplied him by the cook of the *Sheila Grahme*. He filled the kettle with water and set it over the fire. Then he sat down on a rock beside Tomah.

Soon the water in pot and kettle was boiling. Tomah put his piece of salmon in his, David added a little salt. Then he swung

27

his copper kettle to one side and put in enough of the tea leaves to make a stout brew.

Tomah watched his movements curiously, but made no comment.

The fish cooked, it was divided and placed on two pewter plates brought by David, along with two small rounded loaves of corn bread.

When they had finished eating, David poured a tankard full of tea for Tomah and one for himself; adding sufficient sugar, he handed Tomah his, and slowly sipped his own.

David watched him curiously, wondering what his reaction would be to this drink that was utterly foreign to him. But Tomah made no comment until he had finished it, then he said,

"Good drink, P'sazum. Like what we make with Labrador leaves. Any more for Tomah?"

So David poured him another mug of tea. He was about to put in a couple of sugar lumps, when Tomah said:

"*Kadama* (no), P'sazum. Tomah will eat the sugar, after he has finished the drink."

And so it was. He put the lumps of sugar in his mouth, crunching them between his strong teeth. Then, opening the little bag hanging at his neck, containing pipe and tobacco, he filled the bowl, applied a brand from the fire, and smoked contentedly. David did likewise.

An hour later they were again on the way. By mid-afternoon they came to the mouth of the Siks-ta-haw where they found a wigwam set up, and an Indian and his squaw smoking salmon over a wooden frame set over a small fire.

They paused a few moments to speak to them. Moving on, Tomah said, "That is where a sagûm of the Mohawks, and a sagûm of the Maliseets, made a big fight a long time ago. They fought all afternoon with stone knife and axes. Maliseet Chief killed him. So my people always call it Siks-ta-haw. That means killed him."

David remembered having heard the legend a long time before; but he did not say so to Tomah. For he knew that Indians, as well as whites, do not like to be told that the story they have related is well known to the hearer.

Landing at a little spring brook to get a drink of water, David told Tomah how much he was enjoying the journey. "You know, my father, from the time I left you at Casco and landed in *Kam-nok-ik* (England), until I arrived a week ago at the river's mouth, I have known crowds of people. Indeed, I could not count them all during a whole moon."

"Ah," said the Chief, "too many; hard to follow trail of enemy; too many feet; Tomah would not like that."

David couldn't repress a smile at the vision of his Indian friend trying to follow the trail of some particular enemy along crowded Aberdeen or London streets. He said gently, "That is true, my father; there are too many feet."

An hour before nightfall they stopped, lifted the canoe from the water and laid it bottom-up on a grassy sward a few rods from the brook. Another fire was laid, more salmon cooked, more tea made.

They cut fir boughs and made a mattress with them, beneath the canoe.

When darkness fell they sat beside the campfire; sometimes in conversation, again lapsing into a mutual silence that lasted a long while, each wrapped in his own thoughts. For there is nothing more conducive to silence and retrospection among friends than a little woodfire in the out-of-doors: birch, and maple, and pine, whose varied saps, distilled in Nature's laboratory, are released in fragrant smoke to rejoin the elements that had gone into their making. It is this mysterious bond that drew men together in that far age when one of their number first made a little fire, and his tribesmen gathered about it, their hearts filled with awe and admiration at this strange and beneficent God conjured from a few pieces of wood.

The moon rose, pursued its age-old course. It shone on the river, lighting up the shallow water that danced in tiny waves over the bar. Occasionally, a salmon leaped out of the silvery ripples, to fall back with a resounding splash. Save for the river rippling over the bar, or the infrequent call of some night bird, or when a stick fell into the coals, sending up a shower of miniature stars, profound and impressive silence brooded over the scene.

And sitting there, David Cameron knew that for league upon league there was no habitation of man save the bark wigwams of the Indians, and at Medaweska, the rude log cabins the harassed

Acadian refugees had reared, in the hope that at last they had found a permanent abiding place.

But remembering that New Englanders had already surveyed a township on the lower river, he knew that it was only the forerunner of a general exodus that would eventually spread ever upwards along this noble river of the Maliseets.

As though he had known his companion's thoughts, Tomah removed his pipe from his mouth and spoke, "Quebec she fall, Beauséjour she fall, Men-ah-quesk she fall, Louisburg she fall. English hold all the forts. *P'l-etch-e-min* (French) not fight any more. *Kadama* (no). *Boston-keo-e-uk* (Boston people) they come up the river to St. Ann's, start to measure ground for a town. What did we do, P'sazum? Well, all our warriors from Medowktek and Ek-pa-hawk put on the war paint, go down the river, tell *Boston-keo-e-uk* go back; that is our ground. *Ah-ha*; what do you think? They go; hurry quick. *Ah-ha*, English conquer *P'l-etch-e-min*, but they not conquer Maliseets in war.

"They tell us to come to Halifax and sign Treaty of Peace. We go. White father gave us big feast, open barrel of wine. *Ah-ha*, maybe he think it drown our heads, and we not know what we do. But we have the Treaty read to us, and what we not like we have crossed out, and put in what please us.

"When it is all right, we sign Treaty with our totem mark, and make peace with them. But they did not keep their promise to send our priest back to us. Not yet. Maybe he come later. And I tell you, my son, if the English come up the river above St. Ann's, we will make war. *Ah-ha*, Wul-ahs-tukw belongs to Maliseets a long time before the *P'letch-e-min-uk* (Frenchmen) come to the mouth of the river in big canoes with wings like great bird. We made friends with them. Always they treat Indians like brothers. But English they come too many. They look at us cold and say, 'This now is our country. We win it from the *P'letch-e-min*.' *Ah-ha*, but they not win it from Maliseets—not yet."

He had been speaking vehemently. Now he ceased. Refilling his pipe, he lighted it with a brand from the fire and smoked in silence, his dark eyes fixed with brooding intensity at the leaping flames, his fine features immobile as a mask.

For a few moments the Scot made no remark. Finally, touching his companion's arm, he said gently, "Tomah is P'sazum's father and friend. His son knows his father is wise. Perhaps Tomah will learn that it is the wish of the English to be just. But because I love you, I ask you not to take up the hatchet, no matter how unjust their demands. For the English are as many as the leaves on the trees. They would destroy Tomah and his people."

Slowly the Chief removed his pipe from his mouth, and turning to David, said, "My son has an old head on young shoulders. What he has said is true. But is it not better to die, than be a slave? Tomah does not know. He will think it over. Tomah will now sleep."

They spread their blankets on the ground beneath the upturned canoe and stretched out, feet to feet, as they had done scores of nights in other years. But, although David closed his eyes, sleep did not come for a long while. The conversation just ended, Tomah's assurance that his people would fight if the English ventured above St. Ann's, disquieted him. For he knew that further progress of the New Englanders up the river was inevitable; as inevitable as that day would come on the morrow.

In later years, he was to learn that his forecast had come true. For following the disbandment of the Loyalist American regiments that had fought during the Revolutionary war, they had come in thousands to the river of the Maliseets and settled on the land; even as far north as the Great Falls, Chic-seen-i-beg, more than ninety leagues from the river's mouth.

And he learned how the English Commissioners had come in a canoe up the river to Medowktek, to tell the Maliseets there to move on. Then the aged Tomah appeared, surrounded by his tribe. His wrinkled cheeks were daubed with red ochre; his war bonnet was upon his grey locks; about his neck the silver medal given his father by the great Count Frontenac, and a wide silver bracelet on each arm.

Drawing himself to his full height, he asked the Commissioners their mission. And their leader said, "By what right do you hold this intervale of Medowtek?"

Then Tomah half turned, and pointing with a majestic gesture to the little cemetery beside the chapel, he said in a ringing voice that awed his hearers: "There lie the bones of our fathers. There lie the bones of our children. It is enough!"

But of this David Cameron knew not, as he courted sleep a long time before it finally came to him that night, following his first day's journey from Medowktek. For the scheme was taking form in his brain—a great enterprise that was to allay the resentment of the Indians to the inevitable expansion of the English up their river, and would also be the dominant factor in a more lenient policy that would allow the Acadians once more to settle along their beloved shores.

10

The following day Tomah and David came to the mouth of the Na-goot, up which the silver salmon in untold numbers go to spawn, even to the far waters of the Nalaisk* and the Mamozekel;* and the Na-goot-sis,* (which means the little Na-goot) where one may see the towering peak of the mountain known to the Indians as the Great Sa-gûm-o.*

Three miles farther on they passed the Lustook;* then, on their right, the Pulam,* or Salmon River, where Tomah speared a goodly fish.

Five more leagues and the water swiftened, so that Tomah had to bend his shoulders to the setting pole. Finally, David could hear a deep rumbling, and knew they were nearing the great falls of Chic-seen-i-beg. (Which in the Maliseet tongue is said to mean a destroying giant).

They reached the foam-flecked basin a half mile below the falls, and landing, portaged the canoe, and what supplies they could carry, by a path the Indians have used from time immemorial to reach the river above the cascade.

There they found the remains of a bark wigwam. Tomah said it was a very old *K-ne-wi-godik* (camp-ground). But he suggested they go up the river a mile beyond the noise of the falls, and use their canoe for a tent as before. Therefore they went back to the basin, and, returning with the remainder of the luggage, reloaded the canoe and departed to the place Tomah had proposed.

That night there was a heavy rain accompanied by thunder and lightning; but they slept dry and well, rose at daybreak, ate breakfast, and continued their journey.

They were now about twelve leagues from Medaweska. Tomah said they would reach it in five or six hours. But shortly before midday the canoe began to leak. They landed; barely had they mended it with pitch, mixed with ashes, when another thunder storm came up that lasted until nightfall.

An hour after sun-up they were again on the way. This day the air was much cooler, so David got out his warm plaid and wrapped it about his shoulders and middle.

During the last few miles of their journey he often found his heart hammering with excitement, as he tried to envision the manner of his reception by the father and daughter he had not seen for more than a decade. Of course she would not remember him. He had been a lad of sixteen, she a girl of twelve. His lips framed a dozen sentences he would use by way of introducing himself, so that finally they tumbled about higgledy-piggledy in his head, like beans in a kettle.

At noon they landed, made a fire, and broke their fast. Here, after shaving, David carefully combed his red hair—those locks that had been the cause of amusement to Indian tribes from Virginia to Medowktek. Then, from his knapsack, that contained, besides other things, a small box of medicines, he took out a fresh ribbon and carefully tied it in a bow-knot about the hair he had twisted in a queue at the nape of his neck. Now, with a final look at his face in his little mirror, he told himself he wished he were less plain.

But though he had never thought so, David Cameron was far from plain. And here I feel it is just to him to describe his personal appearance at this time of his life, as well as the dominant characteristics that ever distinguished him in all his dealings with men. His features were rugged, slightly tapering from a high forehead to his strong chin; and, though serious in repose (for he was a man of deep thought), when he was amused, or animated, his whole face lightened and his grey eyes twinkled. He was well above middle height, spare of frame and muscular.

He was modest and gently tolerant of the foibles of others. But his personal integrity was so great that, once convinced in his own mind that a course was right to pursue, or to abstain from, no argument of his fellow men, nor any offer of emolument was sufficient to induce him to change it. For this some have called him a dour Scot; but I, who have known him best of all the world—save perhaps his wife—know that no man was more generous in admitting an error of judgment.

11

And so, re-seated in the canoe, David finally turned to Tomah and again said, "My father, you are *quite* sure Mademoiselle Chartier is not married?"

"She was not married when I came from Quebec," repeated the Chief.

"But of course she may be promised to wed," pursued David.

The Chief lifted his pole, then, as he thrust it against the bottom, said, "Tomah does not know."

"Of course not," conceded David, and added, "You say she is *wul-e-go* (she looks nice)?"

"*Ah-ha*, my son."

"And is she tall, or short, my father?"

"She is not tall; nor is she short. Mademoiselle she comes a little higher than P'sazum's shoulder," answered the Chief. "What does that matter, my son?"

"Oh, it doesn't, really," said David earnestly; and more to himself than to Tomah, "I remember her eyes are brown."

And Tomah said, "Like beech nuts, when the frost makes them fall from the trees." After a few moments silence, "You want *Nuks-qa P'l-etch-e-min* (young French woman) for your wife, P'sazum?"

"Yes," answered David, "that is why I came up the river. But, my father, I know not if she will have me."

"Ask her, my son. If she say 'no', pick her up in your arms, put her in the canoe. We will go down river quick. Her people will not catch Tomah. Bye and bye she will say, *Ah-ha*, P'sazum, I take you for my man.'"

David knew that Tomah was wholly serious, therefore he did not laugh. To do so would have wounded the Chief's pride. So he merely said, "My father, I could not do that. Besides, an unwilling servant makes but a sad housekeeper."

"*Ah-ha*," said Tomah. "My son is wise. In old time," he continued, "when young *skigin* (Indian) see a young woman that know how to make moccasins, cook salmon, and meat, sew bark on canoe, and fill in snowshoe frames with caribou or moose string, he went to her father's wigwam with a wood chip in his hand. He throw it in her lap. If she like him for husband, she pick up chip and smile at him. But if she not like him for husband, she look cross, and pick up chip and throw it back of her on floor of the wigwam. Young *skigin* leave. Bye and bye he find a young woman that smile when he throw a chip in her lap. Then *he* happy. *She* happy. *Ka-loo-ut* (good)."

"There are different customs in different countries," said David gently. "I will ask Mademoiselle, and abide by her answer, be it good, or ill. But, my father, now that we are nearing Medaweska, I confess I am nervous. When we were far off, I was brave."

"*Ah-ha, P'sazum*," said Tomah; "just like young *skigin* when he dance first war dance. He think then how many of the enemy he kill and take their scalps. When he starts on the warpath he is brave too. But when he gets close to enemy warriors, he feels bad in his stomach, like when he not have anything to eat for three, five days."

At this David laughed heartily. He said, "My father, that is exactly how *I* feel, even though *I* ate only a short time since."

12

David Cameron would never forget his first view of the little Acadian settlement. It was set in a pine grove in the angle formed by the Medaweska and the Saint John. Smoke came from the stone chimneys; a few canoes were drawn up on the beach. At first he saw no sign of man, woman, or child. But presently, as they drew nearer, a little boy came to the door of one of the cabins. He stood there a few moments, then disappeared within. A man and a woman came out, stood with hands shading their eyes intently gazing at the oncoming canoe, now three or four hundred yards distant.

David was conscious that his heart was pounding in his throat. Could the man and the woman be Monsieur Chartier and his daughter? He thought not. The woman was buxom, and the man much shorter than his memory of Monsieur Chartier.

He saw the man turn his head towards the other cabins. But, though David could hear no words, it was quite evident that he had called to the others; for almost instantly half a dozen men, and as many women, followed by about twenty children, rushed from the doors and joined them.

His eyes swept over the crowd, singling out the women, hoping to recognize among them the girl he had known as a girl fourteen years before. Finally, he shook his head. She was not there. Was it possible she had gone on to Quebec? His throat felt dry; he found it difficult to swallow. His hands pressed on his knees were shaking; or was it his knees that were behaving so oddly?

The canoe was nearing the shore; only a few more rods and he would land. Men, women, and children had crowded down to the beach.

Tomah eased the canoe into shallow water, stepped out and drew it still closer. David rose to his feet. Just as he did so he saw her.

She came from a cabin to the right of a big pine tree that reared its height far above its fellows. She was dressed in a brown frock with tight-fitting bodice and white collar that came to her shoulders. On her head was a little white cap, the sides flaring away from her ears. Her face was oval, the nose small. She moved with grace, her full skirt swinging as she came towards the beach.

As David stepped out on the pebbly shore, Monsieur Chartier—he knew it was Jeanne's father, even though his hair was now grey, and his face seamed with wrinkles—moved forward until he was only a couple of feet distant.

The Scot removed his hat and held out his hand. "You are Monsieur Chartier?" he said in French.

"Yes, I am Monsieur Chartier."

"Of course you do not remember me. I am the boy, David Cameron, once a captive slave at Medowktek, to whom you were kind on the occasion of your visit there fourteen years ago. I have always remembered it."

The little crowd had formed a semi-circle behind Monsieur Chartier. Jeanne stood on the extreme right. He was conscious of her eyes fixed on him wonderingly.

Monsieur Chartier gravely took David's hand. He seemed slightly perplexed.

"Fourteen years is a long time; and much has happened. I would not have known you, Monsieur Cameron; but since you speak of Medowktek, I now remember an English lad was there… yes, yes, it comes back now. You had been kidnapped from your home in England—no, it was Scotland—and sold to a planter in Virginia. Yes, it all comes back. I was on my way to Quebec with my daughter, who later entered the seminary there." He paused abruptly, and David thought there was a sudden note of consternation in Monsieur Chartier's voice as he added, "Do you come from the Fort at the river's mouth, Monsieur?"

"Yes, Monsieur Chartier; that is, I landed at Fort Frederick a few days ago." He paused, as he saw mistrust and apprehension grow Monsieur Chartier's eyes.

"You belong to the military, then?" asked Monsieur Chartier.

"Oh no," replied David hastily. "I am not a soldier. To be frank, Monsieur, when I left Medowktek years ago—or rather Casco Bay, whither Tomah had taken me to meet the masting ship—I solemnly promised him I would return. Because of war, and other reasons, it was no possible to come until this summer.

"On my arrival at Fort Frederick I hired two Indians to bring me to Medowktek. That was a week ago. There I learned that you were at Medaweska. And remembering you, and…" He stumbled in his speech at this point, told himself he was a ninny, quickly regained his poise and said, "And, Monsieur, wishing again to see you, I asked Tomah to bring me up the river."

Monsieur Chartier nodded. "We are all in very poor circumstances, Monsieur Cameron; but you are welcome to what hospitality we cam extend."

"You are very kind, Monsieur Chartier," said David. "The Chief and I will make camp near the little brook we saw a mile down river. He tells me there is a small lake with a dead water at the head of it. I will do some hunting during our short stay here." He paused again. There had been an absence of cordiality in Monsieur Chartier's invitation that left him painfully embarrassed.

Possibly Monsieur Chartier realized the effect of his words, for he said hastily:

"Monsieur must at least have a meal with us. You are welcome. Besides, I should like to have more talk with you. So come, Monsieur; you will honour us by entering our little cabin." He half turned, saw his daughter standing with the other inhabitants. Taking David's arm, he added:

"You will not perhaps remember my daughter, Mademoiselle Jeanne Chartier. She was only a child at the time of our stay at Medowktek. But come, I will introduce you."

David's heart bounded joyously. Her father had called her Mademoiselle!

Hat in hand, he walked beside Monsieur Chartier to where she stood.

Said Monsieur Chartier, "Jeanne, my dear, our visitor is Monsieur Cameron. It is possible you may remember him better than I did at first."

David bowed gravely to her. The curtsey she made him was all grace. But her eyes showed no sign of recognition. Her voice, thought David, was like a lilting brook, as she said:

"No, I am afraid I do not remember Monsieur Cameron. It must have been a very long time ago that we met."

David smiled. "Fourteen years, Mademoiselle." Her fine brows crinkled. He saw she was mentally calculating. Finally, she said:

"I was at the seminary at Quebec fourteen years ago, Monsieur."

"Ah," he said, "but it was while you were on your journey to Quebec that I met you." Then—for she still looked puzzled— "Mademoiselle, I was the boy who caught trout for you with a fly hook at the mouth of the little brook above Medowktek. The Indians called me P'sazum."

"Oh, yes," she smiled; "I remember *that* occasion. One does not wholly forget events like *that*. For I had been fishing with worm bait, which the trout refused. I was quite discouraged. Then the boy—you—came, and took them so easily with your curious fly hook." And she made him another curtsey.

Now Monsieur Chartier spoke, "My dear, I have invited Monsieur to eat with us." He paused, then added, "I had hoped Etienne would have returned before this with some partridges."

She said, "I shall go now to prepare something, and perhaps Etienne will come presently."

As she departed, Monsieur Chartier turned to the little crowd of men and women who had not yet gone, and presented each one in turn to David. He later remembered the names: Cormier, Cyr, Daigle, Thibedeau, Violette, Richard, and Fournier, with their women and children.

Monsieur Chartier asked Tomah to come to the cabin and eat with them. But the Chief declined. He had food, he told Monsieur Chartier, and would eat on the shore.

Returning to David, Monsieur Chartier said. "Come, Monsieur, we shall go to the cabin."

The cabin, David quickly saw, was made of peeled spruce logs, set one upon the other, the ends of each notched with axe or adze to lock them securely together. The interstices were chinked with moss. The roof was of split slabs of cedar, the ends and sides overlapping to keep out rain or snow. A wide stone chimney protruded above the eaves on one side. The cabin, he thought, would be about eighteen by twenty-four feet. The doorway was in the centre, with a small window on either side of it. Later, he was to find there were two other windows, one at either side of the cabin.

They came to the open doorway. Monsieur Chartier said courteously, "Be pleased to enter, Monsieur Cameron."

David stepped inside. Mademoiselle Chartier was bending over an iron skillet that was hanging from a crane in the wide-mouthed fireplace made of beach stones. She straightened; brushing back a straggling curl from her brow she said, "Welcome, Monsieur Cameron." Hurrying to the far end of the room, she pulled forward a chair cunningly constructed of cedar saplings, and added, "Pray, Monsieur, be seated. The dinner," she smiled, showing her even white teeth, "will not be long."

Monsieur Chartier had taken David's hat and hung it on a wooden peg set into one of the logs of the wall. Now, picking up a birch-bark bucket from a bench near the window, he said, "You will excuse me, Monsieur, I but go to the spring for water."

David saw that there were two bunks in the room. One at the end farther from the doorway, the other against the wall opposite the fireplace. Altogether, it was a primitive abode; but withal it diffused that sense of contentment of which ever four walls partake, when lived in by gracious people.

Jeanne Chartier was taking pewter plates and tankards from the cupboard. She placed them on the table. Picking up a long wooden spoon, she went to the fireplace and began stirring what was in the skillet. Then she swung the crane so that the skillet was not directly over the flames.

She seemed perfectly at ease: quiet and sure in all her movements. Though later, she admitted to David, she had felt his eyes fixed on her, and was all fluttery inside.

Finally, she straightened, and looking at him, said, "You must be hungry, Monsieur. But it is now nearly cooked; and as soon as my father returns, we shall eat."

He smiled. "Tomah and I lunched but little over three hours since. But I admit, Mademoiselle, the smell coming from the skillet has given me appetite."

She smiled in return. "I was afraid it had scorched. It is nothing, Monsieur, but moose meat, an onion, and a few potatoes. We planted the vegetables between the stumps of the trees we cut down to build the cabin. When we first came here we had so little we dug and ate lily roots." She paused, glanced at the window, then added, "I had hoped Etienne would have returned before this with some partridges.

At the name of Etienne, David felt an odd sensation in his chest. Perhaps she sensed his unspoken question for she went on:

"Etienne is Etienne d'Amours. His grandfather was Sieur de Clignacourt, whose seigniory included all the land to a depth of three leagues, on either side of the river, from below Medowktek to the Great Falls."

David nodded. He had heard of the Sieur de Clignacourt as one of four brothers by name of d'Amours who, in the last quarter of the 17th Century, had been conferred large grants on the river. Her words strangely disturbed him. He said hesitatingly, "Has Monsieur d'Amours always lived in Acadia?"

"Oh no, Monsieur, not always. His early education was at Quebec, after which he returned to Acadia; and for some years was my father's assistant at Ah-jem-sec. Later, he was a courier carrying messages between the Governor of Quebec and Monsieur Boishébert, commandant of the forts at Men-ah-quesk and the Nerepis. Then," she paused a moment, her eyes clouded as with pain, "he fought in the Battle of the Plains. After the fall of Quebec he returned to Acadia, and when we fled up here to escape the English, he came too. He…" she paused, and David said:

"Yes, Mademoiselle?"

"Pardon me, Monsieur, I was for the moment dreaming. I was going to say Etienne d'Amours is very brave, very resourceful. No one, save the Indians, knows the waterways and the forest trails better than he."

Again David felt a heaviness in his heart. "Is Monsieur d'Amours young, Mademoiselle?"

She hesitated a moment before answering: "I believe he is thirty years of age, Monsieur."

"And married?" he asked in a casual voice.

"Oh, no, Monsieur, Etienne has no wife."

Just then Monsieur Chartier entered the doorway. Setting the bucket of water on the bench, he turned to David. "It is good water; none better on the river. Will you have a drink, Monsieur?"

"Thank you, Monsieur Chartier."

Jeanne picked a mug from the table, dipped it into the bucket and brought it to him. He rose, took it, and making her a low bow, said:

"Thank you, Mademoiselle." He drank it slowly. Then, returning her the cup, "Ah, it is better than wine or spirits, Mademoiselle."

She nodded. "I think so too, Monsieur. We made some wine of the wild cherries when they ripened a couple of weeks ago. We had no sugar, but we put in maple syrup. Of course it will not have matured for some weeks yet." She ceased, set the cup on the table, picked up the wooden spoon and going to the skillet, poked into its depth. Then, with a satisfied nod: "It is ready, father. Will you please set the skillet on the table?"

He did her bidding. "Now, Monsieur," he said courteously, drawing a bench to the table for David to sit on.

David remained standing until Jeanne had seated herself on the bench opposite, then both he and Monsieur Chartier sat down.

Monsieur Chartier served the stew into the pewter plates and gave one to David. Jeanne passed him a wooden platter containing corn meal cakes such as the Indians at Medowktek, as well as the Deleware tribe with whom he had stayed, often baked on hot stones. She said, "I am afraid it will be long before we have white flour, Monsieur Cameron. Perhaps, in time, if we are allowed to remain here."

"I like corn bread, Mademoiselle," he said, taking one of the cakes.

Said Jeanne, "We planted beans, but the rabbits and groundhogs came in the night as soon as they were above ground, and ate most of them before we had a fence made. We shall do better next year."

He put some of the moose meat in his mouth, and having swallowed it, remarked, "It is very good, Mademoiselle."

"Thank you, Monsieur." Then she added, "I wish Tomah had consented to share our meal. But I know that when an Indian says 'no' he means it, and no amount of persuading will change him. And yet," she gave a little laugh, "I always live in the hope that I can break down their reserve. I—"

She was interrupted by a knock at the door; a man lifted the wooden latch and entered.

He was tall, David noted, dark-skinned, with aquiline nose, piercing black eyes beneath a high forehead, and high cheek bones. The long, curly black hair falling beneath his cap was drawn back of his ears and tied in a knot at the nape of his neck. He was a handsome fellow. He carried a gun, and several partridges in the other hand.

"Oh," cried Jeanne, "it is you, Etienne. And you have had luck! Come, we are just beginning!"

His black eyes softened as they fastened on her face with a look such as a dog gives a well-loved master. Then he glanced at David, coolly regarded him a moment, stood his gun in a corner, and dropped his partridges to the floor.

Monsieur Chartier rose to his feet. "Etienne, this is Monsieur Cameron, who arrived from Medowktek a short time ago."

David, who had also risen, bowed to d'Amours. The latter barely inclined his head, then said coldly:

"Monsieur Cameron does our village honour. I had already heard that Monsieur had arrived." Turning on his moccasined feet, he went to the bench and began washing his hands and face. This finished, he came to the table, seating himself beside Jeanne.

Perhaps by that intuitive faculty which women possess to a greater degree than men, she knew that Etienne regarded the stranger with bitter hostility and suspicion. She began chatting with him, asked him if he had seen any large animals, how far he had travelled since morning, and if there were many beechnuts on the ridges.

He answered methodically: There were many beechnuts on the trees; but it needed a good frosty night to make them fall. He had travelled fifteen or twenty miles. As for moose, he added somberly, he had seen none; only the tracks of a cow and calf moose headed in the direction of the Medaweska. It seemed the big animals had deserted the country.

"Yes," agreed Monsieur Chartier, "that is the general report. It is to be hoped they will return before we have exhausted our present supply of meat. Were the tracks old, or of recent make, Etienne?"

"They were four or five days old," answered d'Amours. "They were being followed by a bear, a big one. But they evidently had out-distanced him, because later I saw where he had turned off the trail, while the moose continued on.

"I came across several lodges where beavers had dammed a brook and caused a dead water. I should say there are a dozen lodges. Perhaps twenty-five or thirty adult beavers, besides the young in the colony." He ceased, and confined his attention to his plate of stew.

He ignored the Scot's presence, neither looking at him nor addressing him throughout the entire meal. Indeed, thought David, the whole room seemed charged with the fellow's dislike and distrust.

13

Following the meal, Jeanne gathered up the few dishes, carried them to the bench beside the door, and began washing them. Monsieur Chartier asked David if he smoked.

"Yes, Monsieur," the Scot answered. Taking out his pipe and tobacco he offered the box to Monsieur Chartier. "Will you try some of mine, sir?"

Monsieur Chartier thanked him, filled his pipe and passed the box back. David turned to Etienne, who had taken out his own pipe. "Will you have some of my tobacco, Monsieur? I believe it is quite good."

"I thank you, Monsieur," said d'Amours with studied coldness. "But mine, too, is good." And he proceeded to fill his pipe with tobacco he carried in a little bag about his neck, as do the Indians.

David made no reply. He was annoyed, not so much at d'Amours' refusal of his tobacco, as at his manner. He turned to Monsieur Chartier. "Monsieur, this is a most attractive place you and your people have selected for a settlement."

"Yes," was the reply. Then sadly, "Although we may not be allowed to remain. One never knows from one day to another what will happen. We thought we were safe at St. Ann's, but…" He paused again. Despite their visitor's frank avowal of his reason for coming to Medaweska, he had had so many evidences of ill-faith on the part of the conquerors, that he was more than a little apprehensive that the Scot might be an emissary sent to command them to report to the commandant of the fort at the river's mouth. Perhaps only by speaking more freely, and from the replies of their visitor, could he arrive at the truth. Therefore, he went on, speaking gently, but with deep feeling. And he recounted what he knew of the massacre

49

at St. Ann's during the winter of 1759. David listened, stealing a glance now and then at Jeanne; conscious of d'Amours regarding him intently, and of his puffing nervously at his pipe.

When Monsieur Chartier had finished, David said, "I have heard of that atrocity, Monsieur. But I am sure such wanton acts are deprecated by most of the English race."

"I can believe it, Monsieur Cameron," said Monsieur Chartier. "And I hope you will pardon me for recounting it; and if I now explain why we are here at Medaweska. You must know that during the autumn previous to this happening, a force of fifteen hundred New Englanders, under General Monckton, came up the river to a few leagues above Ah-jem-sec. They burned houses, and killed or drove off cattle and other live stock. They were able to take a few prisoners; but most of the inhabitants escaped to the woods. I had had news of their coming and, with Jeanne and my servants, we fled up the river to Ek-pa-hawk. Finally, a little over a year ago, having intelligence that it was the intention of the New Englanders to settle the lower river, I gathered together a few of my people and proceeded to this place. We had little to bring; a few panes of glass for windows, saws, axes, pewter dishes, iron pots, and the clothes on our backs. Our two cows were led along the beach, or through the woods flanking it, fording or swimming tributary streams as we came to them. Ah, Monsieur, your people do not know what it is to have suffered as have our Acadians." He paused, picked up a brand from the fireplace, and relighted his pipe.

Then David said, "Monsieur Chartier, I do not know if you have heard of the Great Jacobite rising in my country in 1745, with the aim of putting Charles Edward Stuart on the throne of England and Scotland. At that time I was a slave in Virginia. Later, on my return home, I heard all the horrible details of what happened following the battle of Culloden, when the clans were defeated. The Duke of Cumberland marched his troops—many of them foreign mercenaries—throughout the length and breadth of the Highlands. Our people were hunted from place to place. Their houses were burned. It was made an offence, punishable by fine, imprisonment banishment, or death, for any one to wear our beautiful Highland costume. I tell you this, Monsieur, in answer to your remark that my people do not know suffering. But that is past, even though memories of those days still rankle in Scots' hearts. We are now at peace. Let us hope too—now that war between English and French in this country has ceased—that eventually the victors will pursue a more humane and lenient policy; and when, as I trust, your fellow Acadians return, the two races will live in permanent friendship and understanding."

At this Etienne d'Amours laid his pipe on the table, got to his feet, and coming in front of David, said passionately, "Monsieur, you have said the English Government proscribed the wearing of the Highland dress. How was it, then, that the Highland Regiment at Quebec wore this costume? I saw them myself. *'Les sauvages d'Ecosse'*, *'Les petites jupes'* we called them. How do you account for this, Monsieur?" he demanded.

"That is easily explained, Monsieur d'Amours," said David gently. "It was this way: More than a decade after Culloden, the English prime minister, Mr. William Pitt, decided on a more enlightened policy regarding the Scots, with the result that a battalion of some fifteen hundred men was recruited by the Honourable Simon Fraser—a relative of mine, by the way—and they were allowed once more to wear their national costume. Those were the men you saw at Quebec, Monsieur."

If David had thought his explanation would quiet Etienne d'Amours he was mistaken. The fellow went on:

"Monsieur, we know not if what you have said is true." After a momentary pause, he hastened on. "You say the war is over, Monsieur Cameron! But after Quebec fell, what happened, eh? Doubtless Monsieur is quite familiar with the fact that some two hundred Acadians, who had struggled through the wilderness from their place of exile in the American colonies to Quebec, *did* take the oath of allegiance to your English king. How, securing certificates to this effect from Judge Grahme, and with the consent from your General Monckton to settle on this river, they came five hundred miles by canoe and portage to Fort Frederick, and reported to the commandant.

"You know what happened, Monsieur: that the commandant would not credit their certificates as genuine; that he put them on board two ships; sent them to Governor Lawrence at Halifax. From there, this vile governor, who had been responsible for the exile of our compatriots, shipped them to England. What have you to say for this, Monsieur?"

David felt stunned by the fellow's vehemence. It was as though he were accusing *him* of complicity with this act. He could have reminded him how, only little more than half a century before the general Acadian expulsion, Count Frontenac was ready to carry out a plan approved by the king of France, which had for its purpose the conquest of New York. Any of the Catholic faith were to be allowed to remain if they took the oath of allegiance. Citizens wealthy enough to pay ransom were to be imprisoned until they produced the required sum; and all lands in the colony, except those of Catholics, were to be granted to French officers and soldiers. All English and Dutch inhabitants—men, women, and children—were to be dispersed in New England, Pennsylvania, and other places, in such a manner that they could not congregate to recover their property; and, so that the conquest might be more complete, the settlements in New England nearest the French were to be utterly destroyed; while heavy contributions, similar to those demanded by the Iroquois from their defeated rival tribes, were to be exacted from more distant hamlets and towns.

But he had not come to Medaweska for the purpose of making comparisons that could lead only to endless argument. And the fact that the French under Frontenac had first conceived such a plan, and would have put it into effect had they been able to do so, was no excuse for the merciless act of Lawrence and his advisors in deporting the Acadians sixty-four years later.

He was conscious that Jeanne had stopped her work, and now stood beside d'Amours, her beautiful eyes filled with dismay. He said, "Monsieur d'Amours, I assure you I knew nothing of this act of Arbuthnot's until now. I am shocked and grieved; but I feel almost sure that he felt he was justified in doing what he did—ill-advised as it was."

"Hah," cried Etienne, "you try to excuse him! You are like all the English. You—"

He was interrupted by Monsieur Chartier. "Etienne," he said, mildly but firmly, "Monsieur Cameron is at present our guest! As such he is entitled to our courtesy."

A knock sounded at the door. He went to it. It was an Acadian, Monsieur Daigle, come on an errand. Excusing himself to David, Monsieur Chartier passed out, closing the door behind him.

Etienne was silent. For a few moments he stood there, his face working with emotion, then he followed Monsieur Chartier.

Jeanne turned to David, and, her fingers on her lips, whispered to him, "I am so sorry this has happened, Monsieur. You must forgive Monsieur d'Amours his wild outburst."

"Thank you, Mademoiselle. I can quite understand Monsieur d'Amours' feelings." Changing the subject, he said, "After leaving the convent school at Quebec, did you live constantly at Ah-jem-sac and Ek-pa-hawk before coming here, Mademoiselle?"

"Oh no, Monsieur; not constantly. I was at Quebec twice after that. Once for three months, when I was nineteen, and again, during the winter, following the expulsion of our people from Nova Scotia. I was then twenty-two years of age."

"You have relatives there, Mademoiselle?"

"Oh yes, Monsieur; several. You must know that, almost ninety years ago, the Sieur de Soulanges held the seigniory that included Ah-jem-sec. He had married Marie Françoise, a daughter of Monsieur Chartier de Lotbinière, to whom anciently we were related by blood ties. Their daughter, Louise Elizabeth, was born there, and at the age of seventeen married the Marquis de Vaudreuil. He was much older than she, some thirty years, but I believe they were quite happy. It was at the palace of their son— the late governor—that I visited. On the other occasion, I was a guest of Madame St. Claud at the Augustine Convent. She, too, is a relative."

And David thought: Here is an ordinary girl, but one allied to many of the aristocracy of New as well as of Old France. Moreover, her parents had seen to it that she had been well educated. She spoke easily, her voice cultured, her manner without embarrassment.

"That is very interesting, Mademoiselle. Your life at Ah-jem-sec must have seemed quite dull after the gaieties of Quebec?"

Her fine eyes clouded. "Ah, yes, Monsieur. The life there was gay—too gay. The Intendant, Monsieur Bigot, and a hundred others, re-enacted the iniquities of the Court at Versailles. I found there false values; that men and women worshipped money more than they did God; and social position more than virtue. A few were exempt from the demoralizing debauchery—including the governor, Monsieur de Lery, Monsieur LaCorne, Monsieur de Beaujou, and some others. Indeed, Monsieur, both at France, and at Quebec, the nation was corrupt and divided. And like a noxious disease it harboured and bred its final defeat. Oh Monsieur, I can never, *never* forgive them!" David's obvious interest seemed to encourage Jeanne to continue:

"Of course, Monsieur, I had much enjoyment. I loved to dance; and there were many parties held at the palace. You must know that the palace, which is a large stone building, is an impressive place, and on the side overlooking the river is a long gallery. I used often to walk there and view the great rushing tide, and the lights of the ships and the stars reflected on the water; and the Lévis shore. I enjoyed the sight of the soldiers when they mounted guard, both at the gate, and in the courtyard; and the beating of the drums and the presenting of arms when the governor went in or out. Everything was old and historic, not as old as in France, or in your own country, Monsieur, but Quebec was the gateway to New France, and is charged with beauty and romance.

"And then, Monsieur, the church services—I much enjoyed *them*. The governor had his own chapel in the palace, where I heard prayers with him and his family. But often we went to mass at the Church of the Récollets, which is very near to the palace.

"And oh, Monsieur"—her eyes lightened and she was like a young girl as she went on—"I did so delight in the journeys we took that winter about the town, and in the dinners at the seigniories of particular friends of the governor. We went in carioles[§] with two horses, tandem fashion. The carioles of the servants who accompanied us had only one horse. One time we went as far as Trois Rivières to stay two or three days with Monsieur de Rigaud— governor of the town—and his wife. This Monsieur de Rigaud was a cousin of Monsieur de Vaudreuil." She paused, and David said:

"Mademoiselle, do you know, I firmly believe that this Monsieur de Rigaud was the same French officer who captured Fort Massachusetts, after I had been made prisoner by some of his scouts! At any rate, that officer was very kind to me. Perhaps you may remember my telling of it that night at Medowktek fourteen years ago?"

"Only vaguely, Monsieur. But what you say is most interesting," and she smiled at him.

"Will you please to tell me more about your stay at Quebec?" he asked.

"Oh Monsieur, it would take too long. I can only say that my memories of it are both gay and sad. Frankly, I was happy to return to my beloved Wul-ahs-tukw; or, as we call it, Saint John River. You must know, Monsieur, that I am an Acadian."

He nodded. After a short pause she continued:

"My mother had died shortly after my return from the convent school; and, although he would not admit it, my father needed me to look after him."

"Not every daughter would consider that their duty, Mademoiselle."

"That is unfortunate, Monsieur. But I love my father. He is everything to me," she said simply.

He made no immediate comment; but he thought: She will never leave her father. She will feel it her duty never to leave him.

She was speaking. "When peace is finally declared between the two countries, we shall very probably stay here at Medaweska, if we are allowed to do so. But, Monsieur, as my father said to you, we do not know from one day to the next what will happen. We can only hope for the best."

14

What went on outside David learned long after. It seems that the Acadian, Joseph Daigle, had come to borrow Monsieur Chartier's adze. It was in a little bark lean-to at the back of the cabin. Monsieur Chartier told Monsieur Daigle to go take it; and, as he departed, Etienne d'Amours came out and joined him.

He drew him some distance away from the cabin. Then he said, "M'sieu, the Englishman does not tell the truth; he is come to spy on us. He will return, and within two weeks we shall see soldiers come up the river to take and send us into exile."

"No, no, Etienne," protested Monsieur Chartier, "you are wrong. I feel sure it is as he says: that he has come to Medaweska to renew an acquaintance begun long ago. He was a lad of fifteen. It seems he was much affected by what he says was our kindness to him on that occasion. He later returned to his own country."

Etienne gave an incredulous laugh. "So, he came across the sea to give M'sieu thanks, heh? It is a pretty tale! Indeed, it is quite sentimental and romantic!"

"Actually, he came to see Chief Tomah—" began Monsieur Chartier.

"Hah!" interjected Etienne, and laughed again. "That is more marvellous still, M'sieu. He comes across the ocean to see an Indian! It is preposterous!"

"You do not understand," said Monsieur Chartier patiently. "It seems, Etienne, that he and the Chief had been slaves in Virginia on a tobacco plantation. They escaped together, were separated; the boy had a series of harrowing adventures, and finally arrived at Medowktek several weeks ahead of Tomah. It was when I stopped there with Jeanne on our way to Quebec that I met him. Eventually

Tomah took the boy to Casco Bay, where a ship was loading masts for England. He had promised the Chief he would sometime return. He has kept his promise, bringing him a new gun. These, Etienne, are the bare facts."

"It is a pretty romance, M'sieu," said d'Amours. "Since you say so, I believe some of it is true. But the English are a race of liars. They smile when deceit is in their hearts. When I returned from the woods a little while ago, I met Noel Cormier and Joseph Thibedeau. They told me of Monsieur Cameron's coming. They think as I do—that he has come to spy on us, then go back to the fort and tell the commandant we have found refuge here."

"No, no, Etienne, I think you—they—are wrong. The sufferings of our people have made all of us unduly suspicious."

"I will pick a quarrel and kill him," muttered d'Amours.

"Then," said Monsieur Chartier with calm conviction, "the authorities at the fort, who know he came up the river, would send a force to investigate the reason for his failure to return. You forget that the Chief is with him."

"I will kill *him* too," snapped d'Amours. "Tomah deserves to die anyway, for did he not go to Halifax and make a treaty of peace with the English?"

"Yes, that is so. It was necessary. But actually, Tomah, like all his tribe, loves the English as little as we do. No, my friend, none of us must do either of them any harm. Look here, Etienne, I want you to promise me that you will refrain from doing Monsieur Cameron any injury. Remember, my friend, it would bring retaliation and disaster on us all. Jeanne—"

"Has he come to see Mademoiselle Jeanne too?" asked Etienne.

Monsieur Chartier laughed lightly. "That is amusing, Etienne. Monsieur Cameron is doubtless already wedded. At any rate, even if he were not, he is very rich, and you know, my friend, how poverty-stricken we now are. Now, Etienne, I desire your promise—for the good of us all—that you will do him no injury."

For a few moments Etienne d'Amours made no answer. His face worked with conflicting emotions. Finally he spoke. "For Mademoiselle Jeanne's sake I promise, M'sieu."

"Thank you, Etienne," said Monsieur Chartier, and seizing d'Amours hand he wrung it heartily. "Come, let us go in."

But Etienne d'Amours turned off near the door and went to his own little log but beyond Monsieur Chartier's.

Entering the cabin, Monsieur Chartier found David on his feet, hat in hand, and ready to depart. Said Monsieur Chartier, "You are not going so soon, Monsieur Cameron?"

"Yes, Monsieur Chartier." And David smiled. "I have already kept Tomah waiting a long time. I know he is anxious to set up our little wigwam and gather firewood before dark. As I said before, we shall remain a few days, do some hunting, perhaps catch some trout. They again begin to take well at this season of the year." He turned to Jeanne. "Mademoiselle likes trout."

"Yes, Monsieur."

He turned to his host. "May I come again, Monsieur Chartier?"

"Monsieur is welcome," answered Raoul Chartier, and took the hand David extended.

Then, thanking him for their courtesy, David Cameron bowed to father and daughter, and going out, went to the beach and found Tomah.

Tomah, pipe in mouth, was sitting before a little fire he made with some drift wood. He rose to his feet:

"Is the *Nuks qa* (young woman) married, my son?"

"*Kadama* (no)," answered David.

"*Ka-loo-ut* (good)," said Tomah. Then added with conviction: "Some day my son will throw a chip in her lap. She will pick it up and smile at him, and my son will know she wants him for her man." After which pronouncement, Tomah lifted his canoe and gently set it in the water.

15

The brook beside which David and Tomah set up their little wigwam was not big. It emerged through a small ravine it had worn through the bank in ages past, and finally rushed with joyous abandon a hundred feet or more down the sandy beach to blend its cool waters with the great river.

That night David was long getting to sleep. The events of the afternoon, from his landing and his meeting with Monsieur Chartier and his daughter, to the time of leaving the cabin, recurred to him again and again.

As a boy he had not thought of her being "pretty" as lads usually do of girls who have caught their fancy. She was more than that! She was beautiful, not only in person, but with a radiant, spiritual "something" that set her apart, had made her an object of his boyish worship.

He had carried the mental picture of her throughout the years, from that far-off day when first he saw her seated beside her father in the little chapel at Medowktek. He had been able to recall everything: the pure oval of her face; the fair skin relieved by the faint colour in her cheek; the hair that curled in chestnut waves from beneath the little velvet cap; the lace collar on her brown woollen bodice; the sun from the east window enhancing her loveliness.

She was the same, save that womanhood had matured her girlish beauty. He had glimpsed sadness in her eyes. And what people had more cause for sadness! But as the sun bursting through clouds transforms a sombre landscape, thus did some sudden gladness or whimsy enlighten her eyes, so that her whole countenance was transfigured.

He thought of Etienne d'Amours: his dark, handsome face; his brooding hatred of the English, so ready to break into flame;

of his apparent distrust of him. Of course he was in love with Mademoiselle Chartier! That was natural, as was his hatred of those responsible for the defeat, exile, and the irresponsible butchery of his people at St. Ann's.

Did Jeanne love him? He did not know. She had been warm in her praise of him. But it was difficult for him to imagine a girl of her refinement loving a man of his violent nature. And yet, even women such as she often did.

After some hesitation, he decided he would not go to her home on the morrow, despite Monsieur Chartier's invitation. Anyhow, it had followed his own enquiry if he might call again; and Monsieur Chartier, being a gentleman, and courteous, could have made no other answer.

He heard Tomah ask, "Is the bed too hard, P'sazum?" and knew the Chief was aware of his wakefulness.

"Perhaps a few more boughs would be better, Tomah."

"We will get them tomorrow," said the Chief. A little later David sank into a sound sleep.

When finally he awoke the sun was high in the sky. He heard the crackling of fire and looking out saw Tomah seated beside it, smoking his pipe. He had placed over the flames the little kettle filled with water, which was boiling merrily.

David threw off the blankets, and getting up, joined the Chief. He said, "*Wul-e-gis-kit*, my father."

"*Ah-ha*, fine day," agreed the Chief. Then added, "*Ta-ka-o* (cold) when I got up; little frost in the night. Did P'sazum sleep good?"

"*Ah-ha*," answered David, "but it was long coming."

He took out his watch, looked at it, and exclaimed, "Ten o'clock! Well, it seems that what I lost during the first part of the night, I made up later." Observing a pile of boughs near the door of the wigwam, he added, "I see you have cut more boughs."

"*Ah-ha*," said Tomah; "plenty now, my son."

David got his towel from his pack, walked down to the river, and washed his face and hands. As he was drying them he saw fish breaking water at the mouth of the brook. Returning to Tomah he said, "I believe I'll catch some trout for breakfast, my father."

The Chief looked up. "Tomah catch them." He held up four fingers of his left hand. "Plenty for breakfast. Soon be ready for eating." He pointed to the fire.

What David saw was four slabs of wood, two feet long by six inches wide, that Tomah had hewed from a cedar. He had split the trout, fastened them by tail and head to the wooden slabs, and forced one end of each into the sand close to the fire. They were now roasted a lovely seal-brown.

"My father has not been idle," said David, smiling down at the Chief. "He has cut boughs, caught trout for breakfast, cooked them, has water all ready for tea. I will make the tea." So saying, he went to his pack, and returning with the small canister of the precious leaves, he threw enough for their drink into the boiling water. Then he carefully lifted the kettle from the *pichlogun* (the Maliseet name for any sapling or stick used to suspend a kettle or pot over a fire), and set it to one side of the blaze.

Everything now ready, they fell to with a will. After the first mouthful David turned to Tomah. "My father," he said, "your trout are good to my mouth; I have never had better. I thank you."

A pleased look filled Tomah's eyes. "Tomah cooked them in the old-time way," he said, and added, "He knew his son would find them good."

Breakfast over, David and Tomah repaired to the mouth of the brook, and both fishing—Tomah with worm bait, David with flies he had brought with him—they succeeded in hooking and landing twenty fair trout, the largest of which would weigh a pound.

It was near midday when they finally had them dressed. They looked very beautiful, with their carmine and gold spots, laid out on a big grey boulder.

Suddenly it occurred to David to retain six of them, and send the remainder by Tomah to Monsieur Chartier and his daughter. So the Chief got some moss with which he enveloped the trout, covering the whole with birch bark tied about with a spruce root.

He asked Tomah to take them to Monsieur Chartier's cabin. "I shall not go to-day, my father. I am going up the little brook to the dead water you told me about. I may find moose there."

The Chief expressed no surprise at David's decision. He merely said, "It will be as my son says. Tomah will take the fish to the *nuk-sqa* (young woman)."

Before Tomah departed on his errand, he put the remaining trout in moss and bark, and hung the bundle to the top of one of the poles of their wigwam, saying if they were left in the brook an otter or mink on its way to the dead water would surely smell and eat them. Then he picked up his bundle of trout for the Chartiers and walked down to the canoe. David accompanied him to the edge of the water.

As Tomah stepped into the canoe, he held it stationary a moment and said, "My son not get lost. The trail goes along the brook to the dead water."

"Thank you, Tomah," said David. "I promise not to wander away from the water. *Adio*."

16

David watched the Chief's tall form standing slightly forward of the stern, the rhythmic movements of his arms as he lifted and thrust down his setting pole; the impetus of his push lifting the bow out of the water; the little waves that spread fanwise from the stern.

Finally he went back to the fire and, for some of the sticks were still burning, kicked sand over them so that no chance wind would carry sparks either onto their wigwam, or to the nearby forest—now as dry as tinder. Then he got his gun, powder horn and bullets, walked to the high bank, climbed it, and slowly followed the path that Tomah had told him led to the dead water.

He proceeded slowly, and though conscious of the beauty about him, kept a sharp lookout on all sides for possible game. The trees were of enormous size with little under-growth between them; the brook often wound in a desultory manner, now to right, now left, over its boulder-strewn bed, frequently forming still pools as though it would rest awhile to gather energy before pursuing its course.

He was glad he had restrained his desire to go with Tomah to Monsieur Chartier's. But the fact was he did not yet want Monsieur to ascribe his coming to interest in his daughter. That could come later, if at all.

So far the terrain had been more or less level; but presently it began to slope sharply upward, the brook dashing between and over moss-covered boulders, against half-submerged windfalls, rotted with their long immersion. Suddenly he heard from afar the unmistakable sound of a waterfall.

He pushed on slowly, reached a level plateau, and saw it some few rods ahead. He paused, noted that it poured over an almost perpendicular precipice of slate-coloured rock; in its descent striking lichen-covered projections that caused it to fan out like a veil of gossamer. It took his memory back to the waterfall on the little brook at the mouth of which he had caught trout for Jeanne Chartier that far-off day. The Medowktek waterfall was twice as high as this; but no less beautiful and awe inspiring.

Now he approached closer until the spray struck his face in a fine mist. And suddenly, looking across the brook almost opposite him, he saw Jeanne Chartier seated on a fallen log. She was alone. Although her body was facing him, her face was turned towards the cascade, so that she was not aware of his presence.

He gave a whistle and waited, not wishing to cross the brook and possibly frighten her by his sudden appearance.

Evidently she hadn't heard, for she still looked upwards. He tried again, louder this time.

Then she quickly turned her head, and seeing him, rose slowly to her feet.

He slid down the bank, found a boulder, its crest above the water, leaped on it, then to shore, climbed the slope and, hat in hand, approached her.

"Did I startle you, Mademoiselle?"

"No, Monsieur. At first I thought it was a deer that had got my scent. Bears too sometimes give a whistle to call their young."

"You are not afraid of bears?" he asked.

She smiled again. "If I were not armed, Monsieur—but I have my gun with me." She pointed to it, resting against the log.

"That is wise," he said. "Will you not be seated, Mademoiselle Chartier?"

"Yes, Monsieur," and she reseated herself on the log.

He remained standing.

"And you, Monsieur Cameron? There is room for both of us. It is a very big log."

"Thank you, Mademoiselle." Setting his gun against it, he sank down beside her. "Do you often come here?" he added.

"Quite often, Monsieur. It is a beautiful spot. The waterfall fascinates me. You are going hunting, Monsieur?"

"I *was*, Mademoiselle. But if you do not mind, I would much rather sit here with you."

A quick flush dyed her cheek. She looked away a moment, then said, "Did Monsieur spend a restful night?"

"Part of it, Mademoiselle. We had difficulty finding bark for our wigwam. When we did, and had set it up, dusk had come, and we had only time to cut a few boughs for our bed." He was about to add that it was not the lack of boughs that had kept him awake, but refrained. Instead, he said:

"When finally I did get to sleep, I didn't awake until ten o'clock. Tomah had a fire going, had cut more fir boughs, caught four nice trout, which he was cooking, and had water boiling for tea."

She looked up at him. "We much regret, Monsieur, that it was not possible to entertain you for the night. But…" she hesitated. "You saw our accommodations, Monsieur; we have only two beds— if one can call rude bunks such."

"You are very kind, Mademoiselle. But Tomah and I are quite comfortable in our little wigwam. It is near the brook and the river; really a delightful spot."

"Where is Tomah now, Monsieur?"

"Oh—you were not home when he arrived? Of course not; because you would not have had time to reach this place." Then, for she was gazing up at him, a question in her hazel eyes, he went on: "After we had had breakfast, we caught and dressed more trout, so I sent the Chief to the settlement to deliver them to you. He left before I started up the brook."

"You are very good to send us trout. It seems that both times we have met you have favoured us with gifts. I thank you, Monsieur."

"It has been a privilege, Mademoiselle. The first time you were good enough to call me by my Indian name P'sazum." He waited, amazed at his own temerity.

"Oh, Monsieur, that was such a long, long time ago, and I was but a girl. I am now…" He guessed the unspoken remainder to be that she was now a woman, and must observe the proprieties. He said gently:

"It should make no difference, really. Do you remember what P'sazum means, Mademoiselle?"

She smiled. "Yes, Monsieur. You must know I speak the Maliseet tongue."

"That is not the whole of it, Mademoiselle. It is Kul-a-waz-oo P'sazum."

"Of course, Monsieur, I do not remember that that is the rest of your Indian name, but I know it means 'my good star'." Having said it, her cheeks flushed and she looked quickly away. Then carelessly, "It is a very pretty name, Monsieur."

He felt his own face grow hot. He said haltingly, "It *is* pretty, yes, Mademoiselle, and perhaps inappropriate for a man. But as you know, Indians often evince poetic imagérie in their choice of names." He paused a moment. "Would you remember, Mademoiselle, my telling you and your father, and Père Germain, how it was that I, a Scots boy, happened to be at Medowktek?"

"But yes, Monsieur," she answered. That is, I remember that you had been kidnapped, sold as a slave in Virginia, and had travelled hundreds of miles in the company of Tomah, finally to reach the Saint John River."

He nodded, now more at ease, and, pleased that she had remembered so much, he went on. "The ship on which I was put when kidnapped, overhauled a French brig bound from Canada to France. On this French vessel were Tomah and Père Germain. The priest had business in France, and was taking the Chief to see the king. It was a quite common custom, as you doubtless know, Mademoiselle, for the governors of Canada and Acadia to send Indian chiefs to France to see the king. It impressed them with the glory and the might of the monarch, who was pleased to call them his children.

"Well, Mademoiselle, having transferred the rich cargo of furs to our vessel, the English sailors found Tomah in one of the cabins, dragged him on deck, where he broke loose and jumped into the sea. The mate shot at him with a pistol, wounding him in the shoulder, but he was still able to swim. Our English captain ordered the sailors into the longboat to pick him up. He was finally brought to our deck, and taken to the sick bay to have his wound dressed. I did not see him until later.

"Night fell. We poor lads huddled together in the hold finally fell asleep. Some time later a great storm arose, and we were sore frightened, thinking the ship would founder.

"During one of these terrifying moments, when tons of water were hurled on the ship's decks, and the longboat shattered into splinters, the bow lifted so high that I and my poor companions were tumbled backwards, scrambling among the putrid bilge-water.

"It was then that I saw Tomah. He had been brought from the sick bay while we slept, and was bound hand and foot. As best I could I untied his knots. In a few moments he sat up, and in English asked me my name. I told him David. At which he said he would call me 'Kul-a-waz-oo P'sazum,' because I had been a good star to him.

"We became fast friends, Mademoiselle. He taught me many Maliseet words, and when finally our voyage was over, we were both sold to the same planter in Virginia.

"And so, Mademoiselle, that is how I got my name. You must know I look upon the Chief as my second father, and love him as such."

17

When he had ended, she drew a deep breath and said, "It must have been a frightening experience, both before, and during the storm—and you a mere boy!"

He nodded, "Yes, Mademoiselle; but there have been compensations. I…" He was about to add that if he had not been kidnapped and sold into slavery, he never would have met her. Instead, he said, "Have you another name besides Jeanne?"

"Oh yes, Monsieur, two: Marie and Françoise. These were the names of the Sieur de Soulanges' wife, who was a daughter of Chartier de Lotbinière. But I prefer Jeanne best. It was my mother's name."

"All three are lovely. The name Jean is quite popular among our women-folk in Scotland."

"That is odd, Monsieur—I mean the fact that you bestow the name *Jean* on females, which with us is confined to males." Then in a more serious voice, "Are you married, Monsieur?"

The frankness of her question amazed him. He said haltingly, "Oh no, Mademoiselle. Of course I hope to be some day; I have been a bachelor quite long enough."

"Then Monsieur is engaged to wed, is it not so?" And she smiled up at him, her eyes filled with little lights.

"No, Mademoiselle," he replied, "not yet."

"But you know a girl you would like to wed?"

"Yes, that is so, Mademoiselle," he answered in a low voice.

"And have you known her a long time, Monsieur?"

He hesitated a few moments before replying: "Well, Mademoiselle: in one way, yes; in another, no. But I have loved her for very long, and always shall."

"Oh," she said, nodding her head, little imps of mischief in her eyes, "and you have not had the courage to ask her if she loves you?"

"No, Mademoiselle… It requires a great deal of courage."

"Is she beautiful, Monsieur? But, of course she must be! All men think their adored one is beautiful."

"Yes," he answered, "I have seen many beautiful women—but I think *she* is more beautiful than any."

She made no immediate comment. Finally, looking up at him: "Monsieur's adored one must be such a paragon that she frightens him! Well, Monsieur, I think you are unwise to put off for long. I think it must be because Monsieur is very, very shy. It is a most grave fault." And she shook her head at him in gentle reproof.

He nodded. "I am afraid you are right, Mademoiselle. To be frank, I…we…" David paused irresolutely. He had been hurried on so quickly by the flow of her talk; but it was yet too soon to confess that it was *she* whom he wished to wed.

"Yes, Monsieur, go on please; I am much interested in Monsieur's attachment."

"Well," he said lamely, "the fact is, it is wholly a one-sided affair. I mean I do not know if she cares two pence for me. But I hope to find out soon."

"Oh," she said, smiling mischievously up at him, "Monsieur is getting brave!" She ceased and looked away. Poor Monsieur—he was so shy, like a small boy. It was quite obvious he had had little experience with women. And she had been quite shameless in leading him on to reveal purely personal matters. She was about to beg his pardon, when she heard his voice say:

"Would this be yours, Mademoiselle?" and turned to see him holding out to her a little silver shoe buckle.

"Would this be yours, Mademoiselle?" he repeated.

She gazed at it, her eyes wide with astonishment. Then, taking it in her hand, she looked it over very carefully. "But yes, Monsieur!" she exclaimed. "Oh yes, I am quite sure. See: the fleur-de-lys cut into the back; and on the front the initials M.F.J.C.—meant for Marie Françoise Jeanne Chartier. But, Monsieur, how—where—did you find it?"

So he told her how he had come by it, adding: "There it lay all by itself, among the débris on the floor of that little room in the fort at Ah-jem-sec. It was much darkened, Mademoiselle; but I polished it bright with wood ashes, on my way up the river."

She was rubbing a forefinger over its surface, feeling the velvety softness that is a part of all old silver. "It is one of a pair on shoes given me by Madame de Vaudreuil, when I was nineteen. Poor little buckle! It is strange the English overlooked it when they looted the place."

"Yes, that was my thought." He paused with sudden embarrassment. Then, with quick resolve, "Will Mademoiselle be kind and generous, and allow me to keep it?"

A slight flush dyed her cheeks. She said playfully, "Does Monsieur collect ladies' shoe buckles as souvenirs?—Snuff boxes I can understand, and objects of art. But shoe buckles! Oh, Monsieur, that is a curious habit."

He smiled. Then awkwardly, "I cannot add it to my collection, Mademoiselle, because I have made none. But it is never too late to begin. And yours, Mademoiselle, if you will allow me to have it, will be the most treasured." He added earnestly, "Indeed, and indeed, Mademoiselle, it will be the beginning and the end of my collection."

Her heart was playing strange tricks. Yet she said, smiling up at him, "Monsieur is most catholic in his wish to begin and end his proposed collection with but one poor little buckle! There, forgive my banter—Monsieur may have it." Still smiling, she held it out to him.

"Thank you, Mademoiselle. It will be one more memory of you I shall always retain." And he replaced it carefully in his pocket.

At this she dropped her gaze to her hands crossed in her lap. Although she had treated the affair as a joke, she knew it was not *une plaisanterie* with him. His manner, his desire to possess the buckle, his assurance that he would treasure it along with other memories of her, had been said with a sober sincerity, that left her amazed and troubled in spirit. Could it actually be that he was in love with *her*? It seemed incredible. And yet, yes, everything spoke of it: his coming all this distance to renew an old acquaintance; his stilted, boyish embarrassment as he confessed a love he had not yet had the courage to divulge; above all, the look in his eyes when he had said he would treasure her shoe buckle. It was now all clear. He loved her, Jeanne Chartier. He had loved her a long time—from that far day when she had stopped at Medowktek on her way to Quebec!

And she had led him on to talk! Although her enquiry if he were married had been a perfectly natural question, wholly lacking guile, she should have let it go at that. Her face flushed to the roots of her hair, and her heart pounded suffocatingly.

What if he were to go on, declare his love in more specific terms? Then she must hurt him. She shrank from the thought. He was so kindly and gentle. She liked him…yes, more than mere liking. She tried to persuade herself that it was the affection of a sister. For he too had known exile and abuse. Yet she must, soon or late, put an end to it all. Etienne's hatred was not wholly due to the fact that Monsieur Cameron belonged to an enemy race. It was intermingled with mad jealousy of the man who had come such a great distance to see her and her father. Yes, this David Cameron must leave Medaweska. And yet, she didn't want him to go. The sudden knowledge disturbed her, even while her heart joyously exulted in the fact. She was conscious of her hands trembling in her lap. Finally, her composure somewhat regained, she said haltingly,

"Monsieur, I have already told you, but I want to repeat it again, that we…I…very much regret what Etienne said to you yesterday. You were a guest, and we have always treated guests courteously. I—"

"Oh," he interjected quickly, "do not apologize, Mademoiselle. I realized that you were as embarrassed as I was to be the innocent cause of it."

"You are very kind to say so, Monsieur." She hesitated a moment, then, assured in her mind that it must be said, she went on, "Etienne is hot headed. He knows how much we have suffered, he thinks you have come to spy on us, return to the garrison and send soldiers to take us away. But—"

"Good Lord, Jeanne!" he broke in. Then, realizing that he had used her name, he said earnestly, "Pardon me, Mademoiselle, but Monsieur d'Amours, or any others who may think that, do me wrong. It is as I said yesterday. I came to Medaweska for the purpose of seeing two people who had shed light in the heart of a lad who was far from his relatives—for he had no parents living—and had known suffering, perhaps equal to that experienced by your kindred. Tell me please," and he laid a hand on hers clasped in her lap, "that you believe in me?" He was deeply moved and had spoken with some agitation.

Gently she withdrew her hand, and, her eyes on his, said contritely, "Forgive me, Monsieur, I hurt you. It was not meant. What I said was in explanation of Etienne's outburst yesterday. And, Monsieur…" she hesitated. No—she couldn't yet tell him he must leave Medaweska. It would be too much hurt, like reprimanding a child who tenders you a lovely nosegay. She began again: "And now, Monsieur, I hope you will pardon what I said, and know that I do believe in you."

"Thank you, Mademoiselle. Your belief in me means more than I can express in mere words." He paused, then went on, "Mademoiselle, I much want to explain some things that have been greatly misunderstood regarding the expulsion of your French Acadians. The English nation—I mean the home government, Mademoiselle—has been wrongly blamed, and I am afraid always will be, for that inhuman affair. Briefly, it was the descendants of those intolerant Puritans who settled Massachusetts Bay, together with Governor Lawrence of Nova Scotia, who were responsible for it."

She was gazing up at him with wide, incredulous eyes. He went on, "Yes, Mademoiselle, the authorities in England again and again—from the time of Queen Anne, when Nova Scotia was ceded to Great Britain—have advised successive governors to treat the Acadians with kindness and leniency."

"How do you know this, Monsieur?" she asked.

"In this wise, Mademoiselle: I had access to official documents in the Archives in London. They tell the whole story. Even as late as 1755, on the eve of the Expulsion, the Secretary of State himself wrote Governor Lawrence at Halifax, reprimanding him for submitting to them his plan to get rid of the Acadians for all time. But the expulsion was already under way. The letter either arrived too late, or Lawrence ignored its contents. Indeed, the colonial administrators in New England, acting with Governor Lawrence and his advisors, had decided on the expulsion long before. In other words, Mademoiselle, they had been determined on carrying it out for years, prior to putting it into effect. Their excuse was that the Acadians had refused to take an unqualified oath of allegiance to the king. This would be amusing—if the results were not so tragic—coming from a people who, for the most part, almost from the time they had landed in New England, were filled with the seeds of rebellion to the Crown.

"I could go on for hours, Mademoiselle; even citing letters from the successive governors of Nova Scotia to the Lords of Trade in England, and the answers they received in reply. I would now rather talk of other things. But I do want you to know that the English government of that time, which, being a Scot, I have many reasons not to love, were not responsible for the deportation of your compatriots, and that it was wholly the work of colonial administrators." He ceased, and she said:

"Monsieur, I have no doubt whatsoever of your sincerity. But we have been led to believe it was the English government who ordered the expulsion; therefore, I hope you will forgive me, when I say it seems to me incomprehensible that the colonial administrators would go so far as to arrogate to themselves an authority denied them by their king."

"Mademoiselle," he said earnestly, "it is as I have said. I have seen the proofs with my own eyes. I hope that eventually not only you, but all your Acadian people as well, will arrive at the facts of the case as *I* know them."

"I hope so too, Monsieur," she said gently. "As it is, the damage has been done, and the seeds of enmity sown. It could have been otherwise, Monsieur, if, as you suggest, wilful men had not been in control in this land of Acadia."

"We must exempt two governors," he said hastily—"Paul Mascarene, and Mr. Hopson. They understood the Acadians, and were filled with humanity. Mascarene, by the way, was a French Huguenot. And, Mademoiselle, on the very eve of the expulsion, a Colonel Winslow, one of the officers delegated to carry it out, expressed his dislike of the whole business."

She nodded. "I have heard of Monsieur Mascarene. He was a good and brave man. I wish to thank you, Monsieur, for telling me all this."

He smiled down into her eyes. Again the desire to tell her of his love almost overwhelmed him. But he held it in leash. He had come only yesterday; there would be other days. Yet, because he wanted to prolong the hour, to hear her voice, that was like a lilting brook, go on and on, he said:

"Will you please tell me more about Ah-jem-sec, Mademoiselle? The very name Ah-jem-sec fascinates me, as do so many Indian place names."

She returned his gaze, thankful to have the conversation switched to yet another topic less dangerous than love, and said, "Certainly, Monsieur. It will be for me a pleasure to tell you about a place that, despite its remoteness from civilization, as we call it, means so much to me."

18

"It has a most interesting history, Monsieur," she went on, "You must know that there has been a fort and trading post at that place since the time of Cromwell, when the English took over Acadia from our French. It was built by Monsieur Temple, who had been named English governor of the country; and much trade was done with the Indians.

"But some few years later Acadia again became French, and the Chevalier de Grandfontaine, who was governor, sent the Sieur de Soulanges to command at Ah-jem-sec and hold the river against any encroachments of our enemies. The fort was in much disrepair, but he restored it, and he too carried on an extensive trade in peltries.[§]

"But a few years passed by, and while his daughter, Louise Elizabeth was still an infant (she who later was wedded to the Marquis de Vaudreuil), a Dutch pirate entered into partnership with one Monsieur Rhoade of Boston, to ravage the French posts in Acadia. With a crew of a hundred men they sailed up the Saint John River, and, since the Fort had only a dozen men for garrison, they captured it. They dismantled the small cannon and put them on board their ship, then, tearing Monsieur de Soulanges from his wife and child, they sailed back to Boston. This small exploit seems to have justified them in proclaiming all of Acadia Dutch territory, which they renamed 'New Holland'.

"From Boston they sent word to Count Frontenac at Quebec, demanding a ransom of one thousand beaver pelts for the release of Monsieur de Soulanges. Count Frontenac immediately acquainted his government in France of the situation; but it was almost a year before his lieutenant was set at liberty. It is said that the Count paid the ransom out of his own pocket.

"But in the meantime, he sent a party in canoes to the Saint John River, who brought Madame de Soulanges back to Quebec. You know what a great distance that is, Monsieur. It must have been a time of great mental suffering to the poor lady—wondering if ever she would see her husband again.

"On Monsieur de Soulanges' return to Quebec, Count Frontenac decided to re-establish French suzerainty on the river, and the former commander, and his wife and child, returned to Ah-jem-sec, having been given a grant of one hundred square miles of territory, including the fort, and as far up the river as St. Ann's.

"But Monsieur de Soulanges did not remain for long on his domain, going back to Quebec, where his daughter Elizabeth was sent to the convent school.

"Is it not all interesting, Monsieur?"

"Yes, Mademoiselle. Tell me more, please. It is quite fascinating."

"Gladly, Monsieur. I was but afraid I was tiring you. Well, following de Soulanges, the seigniory was granted to Louis d'Amours, Sieur de Chauffours. He would be a brother of the Sieur de Clignacourt, and great uncle to Etienne, whom you met yesterday.

"This Sieur de Chauffours tilled the soil and engaged in the fur trades, as did all his predecessors. His wife, the beautiful Marguerite Guyon of Quebec, was a noble, kindly woman, and was instrumental in securing the freedom of several English lads who had been taken prisoner by the Indians during their raids against the New England settlements.

"It was during this time, Monsieur, that Governor Villebon came to the river to hold it for the king; and while he was building his Fort St. Joseph, at Nashwaak, opposite St. Ann's, he made Ah-jem-sec his headquarters.

"Fort St. Joseph was only completed a little while, when English vessels came with soldiers from Boston, determined to drive our French from the river. They burned buildings, killed cattle and other stock. Monsieur de Chauffours was in France at the time, and his wife and a few retainers, with an English boy her husband had bought from the Indians, fled the place. But before she left, she had this English boy nail up a paper on the door of her dwelling, saying she had been kind to English captives, had already given two or three their freedom, and asked the English commander to spare her possessions.

"This, Monsieur, he did, going up the river to attack Fort Nashwaak. But de Villebon repulsed him, and he sailed back to Boston.

"The destruction of the settlers' homes, followed by the abandonment of the river by its French garrison, left the inhabitants unprotected. They moved away, and for many years Ah-jem-sec, as well as the whole river, was deserted save for the Indians, who occasionally made it a refuge for a few days and nights. Ah yes, Monsieur, Acadia has had a romantic and tragic past." She paused, remained silent for a few moments, her eyes sadly bent on her hands clasped in her lap.

And watching her, David pondered over the changes that had taken place since first the river was discovered by DeMonts and Champlain in 1604. First the French, then English, next Hollanders, again French, had exerted their sway over it. Now again it was English. And the river still flowed in its resistless might to the harbour's mouth, where once stood the palisaded stockade enclosing the bark wigwams of Chkoudun, the Maliseet Chief, and his tribesmen.

Yes, English now. Thousands more would come. A new era was dawning. What changes the remote future would bring none could forecast. For Time, and his handmaidens, the Fates, have a strange way of creating new conditions against which the puny efforts of the conquerors are of no avail!

Jeanne's voice fell on his reverie: "Thirty years ago the old seigniory was leased to my father. He brought my mother there, and engaged heavily in the fur trade. And then I was born. Often Indian families camped nearby. Almost as soon as I was able to walk I played with their children, and learned to speak their language.

"My mother taught me to read and write, and my early childhood was happy. Though when, at long intervals, my mother and father received letters by couriers from Quebec, and I learned I had several cousins my own age, I often longed to make their acquaintance."

Pausing a moment, she said, "I must go, Monsieur. It has..."
She paused again as the crack of a bush behind her caught her ear,
and turned to see Etienne d'Amours, a frown on his handsome
face, standing a few feet distant. She rose to her feet, as did David.
"Etienne!" she exclaimed.

<h1 style="text-align:center">19</h1>

David Cameron bowed to the Acadian. "Are you also hunting this afternoon, Monsieur d'Amours?" he said.

For a few moments the Acadian made no reply. Finally, his face expressing his dislike of the Scot more plainly than words, he answered with studied coldness:

"When a d'Amours hunts, he does not sit by a noisy brook, where he cannot hear animals approaching. I would advise Monsieur to go farther up the stream a half league, where there is a dead water. It is a place deer and moose frequent occasionally. But perhaps Monsieur Cameron does not know the habits of these animals."

"Oh yes, but I do." And David smiled good naturedly. "I lived with the Maliseets two years, and became quite familiar with the haunts of the forest creatures."

Etienne d'Amours scowled. He made a low bow. "Allow me to congratulate Monsieur. I was under the impression the English were more proficient at hunting and scalping women and children, as at St. Ann's!"

"Ah," returned the Scot, "Monsieur d'Amours has, I am sure, been labouring under a delusion; which is all the more singular since he was present at the Battle of the Plains."

His retort had no sooner been out of his mouth than he regretted it. Whatever the provocation, he should have had more regard for the presence of Jeanne Chartier, than to have added fuel to a quarrel that could only distress her.

The dark face of the Acadian had flushed crimson. Then, with a muttered oath, he sprang like a panther towards the Scot.

But quick as he was, Jeanne was quicker. She glided between the two men and caught d'Amours by the sleeve of his fringed deer-skin jacket. "No, no, Etienne," she pleaded, "Remember your promise to my father!"

He did not answer, tried to break away; but she held him firmly. She turned frightened eyes to David. "Go, Monsieur," she pleaded. Then to d'Amours: "Etienne, if you have our interests at heart, do nothing rash!"

He ceased his efforts to break away, and looking down at her, said quietly, "All right, Jeanne. It is all right."

"Thank you, Etienne; thank you," she said gently.

David had half turned to go, but stopped, and turning, said, "Mademoiselle Chartier, I humbly apologize for the part I have played in this lamentable affair." Then to d'Amours:

"Monsieur, if in the heat of argument you were discourteous, it was equally so on my part to remind you of the defeat of a very gallant foe. As for the sad doings at St. Ann's, I had nothing to do with that, and I deprecate the brutality of its perpetrators, that has brought a stain upon all who wear the king's uniform." He paused a moment, then continued, "I came to Medaweska in amity, Monsieur. I am here but a few days, at most, and would depart in amity." He held out his hand. "Will not Monsieur d'Amours take my hand, and let bygones be bygones?"

The Acadian made no reply, nor any effort to accept the proffered hand. He stared at the Scot, his brows drawn in a heavy frown.

Jeanne spoke. "You see, Etienne," she said pleadingly, "he desires our friendship. He says he came in amity. I believe him, and you must also."

The Acadian shook his head stubbornly. "Not so, Jeanne. I will not take the hand of one who belongs to the accursed race that has sent our people into exile, and butchered others in cold blood. Between him and me there can be no friendship." He gazed down at her, a great tenderness in his dark eyes, and added, "Come, Jeanne, allow me to escort you back to our village."

For a moment she hesitated. She half turned her head towards the Scot, standing there, the butt of his gun pressed into the soft moss. He looked hurt at the rebuff to his effort at rapprochement. She said, her voice sweetly sad:

"It is better that Monsieur Cameron leaves Medaweska today—tomorrow, at latest." She paused, added gently in the Maliseet, "*Adio*, Monsieur P'sazum." She turned, picked up her gun. "Come, Etienne," and stepping ahead of him, took the same path by which she had come to the place. Etienne followed, his gun barrel resting in the hollow of his left arm.

For a few moments, until the forest had swallowed them, David Cameron stood where they had left him. Finally, with a look about him at the beautiful waterfall, and the log upon which he had found her seated, he turned, and slowly, sadly, retraced his steps along the brookside to the little wigwam where now Tomah patiently awaited him.

20

For fully five minutes Jeanne and Etienne walked along the woodland path with no words between them. Finally, Etienne spoke, his voice sullen and accusing:

"You sat there and talked with the Englishman, Jeanne! Is it so soon that you can forget the wrongs we have suffered?"

She stopped in her tracks and swung about facing him. "It was a chance meeting, Etienne. True, I sat and talked with him, but—"

"You could so soon forget?" he repeated. "You forget that they killed and scalped Nastasie, wife of Eustache Pare, and their three children; and the wife and child of Michael Bellefontaine! Hah, yes; it is true that the English at Halifax had offered thirty pounds for the scalp of each male Indian above sixteen years of age. But it would be difficult for the authorities to distinguish between the scalp of an Indian and that of a Frenchman, male or female, young or old. Not that it would make any difference to them," he added bitterly. "You forget all this, it seems."

"I forget nothing, Etienne," she said with a shudder. "But," she continued, "this Monsieur Cameron had nothing to do with our troubles. He was far away in his own land. Besides, he is a Scot, not English."

"He belongs to the accursed country!" he cried. "Scots fought us at Quebec—they were devils. But I had my revenge of them!" he added savagely. "When we retreated, some of us got behind trees, and as they ran for us, their little *jupes* (kilts) swinging from side to side, we shot five of them. Ah, it was good to see them fall!"

He paused a moment, then added, "And you, Jeanne, would have me take this man's hand? I would sooner cut off my own!"

"He is leaving Medaweska; you heard him say so, Etienne," she reminded him with sad patience.

"It will be well," he said. And added grimly, "It will be the better for him!"

She nodded. "In the meantime, you must remember your promise to do nothing rash. You know it would bring disaster to all of us."

He swept his hand across his brow. "Yes, yes, Jeanne," he said contritely, "I forget. In my anger I forget. It is my weakness. Only never can I forget that I love you."

She said gently, "We must not speak of that, Etienne. We have talked it all over many times, and you know my answer."

"I will never cease to hope," he told her. He paused. "Is it that you love this Scot?" he demanded harshly.

She gave a low laugh. "What!" she cried, "So soon? He came but yesterday. Do you think he would be leaving in a few days, at most—as he said he was—if he loved me, and knew that I loved him? Come, Etienne, it is time for me to return home and get the evening meal."

She walked ahead of him. And as she went she was troubled in spirit.

21

The following afternoon David Cameron again went to the waterfall. Without knowing why, he felt that Jeanne Chartier would be there. He was disappointed. Perhaps she would come later. Seating himself on the fallen log, he watched the path by which she had come and gone yesterday.

"And yet," he asked himself, "why *should* she come?" She had told him quite plainly it would be better should he leave Medaweska. And had added: "To-day, if not tomorrow, at latest."

There had been a note of finality in her voice and words that at the time had left him in no doubt she had meant what she said.

He had been hurt. For though unbidden, he had come on a friendly errand. And yet, he told himself, he felt sure she had not meant to hurt. For just before leaving she had paused, and said: "*Adio*, Monsieur P'sazum." It had been uttered gently, a little sadly, he thought. Her use of his Indian name a sort of token meant to assure him that she bore him no ill will.

And then, last night, rehearsing the whole affair, there had come to him with a sudden flash of inspiration her reason for dismissing him. And he exulted, told himself he had been a fool not to understand. Certainly it had been because she feared Etienne d'Amours might do him injury.

Well, her "tomorrow, at latest" was now; and he was still here. As for d'Amours—the fellow was a hot-head; ready, it seemed— aye, anxious—to pick a quarrel with him on the slightest pretext. It was quite obvious he was in love with Jeanne Chartier. Perhaps she actually loved him.

But until he knew positively, that she was promised to d'Amours, or to another, he was not going to be hurried away by the fellow's undoubted enmity towards him. Moreover, whatever the issue, he was determined to talk over with Raoul Chartier the plan he had formulated on the way hither of establishing truck houses on the river; not only for his own personal benefit, or for that of Monsieur Chartier. It was bigger than that; wider in its scope; something that, if he were able to put it into effect, would benefit Indians and Acadians alike.

The minutes passed, and he still sat there on the fallen log. A half hour; an hour; two hours went by. He replaced his watch in his pocket. Of course he had been silly to think she would come today. Doubtless she now thought him already on his way to Medowktek.

He picked up his gun, slowly got to his feet; then, as though drawn by a magnet, he turned to see her coming towards him through the trees. His heart raced madly.

He removed his hat, bowed to her. Her cheeks were flushed, her eyes bright. She seemed to him more beautiful, more desirable than ever. She did not betray surprise at seeing him. She said gently, standing in front of him:

"You did not go, Monsieur?" And added in mild reproof, "By now your canoe should be nearing the falls of Chic-seen-i-beg."

He smiled. "Will you not be seated, Mademoiselle?"

For answer she laid her gun against the log and sat down.

"May I also sit, Mademoiselle?"

"Of course, Monsieur."

He sat down beside her, "You did not expect me to go so soon, Mademoiselle Jeanne?"

She smiled, and, looking up at him, said evasively, "I have heard that the English are a very, very stubborn race."

"But I am a Scot."

"It is all the same, actually, is it not, Monsieur?"

He gave a low chuckle. "Scots would thank no one for saying so. Indeed, Mademoiselle Jeanne, we Scots feel quite superior to the English."

"In stubbornness, Monsieur David?" And he noted that having accepted without protest his calling her "mademoiselle Jeanne," she now called him "monsieur David." They were getting on.

"In everything, Mademoiselle Jeanne." After a brief pause, "You have not answered my question, Mademoiselle."

"Oh, you mean did I expect you to leave Medaweska?"

"Yes, Mademoiselle Jeanne."

"You are most persistent, Monsieur David." She hesitated a moment. Then with heightened colour, "No, Monsieur, I did not think you would go."

"Why?" he asked.

She crossed and uncrossed her hands in her lap. "Because, Monsieur, you are both persistent, and—stubborn."

He gave a low laugh. "That is what my partner, Ian Grahme, has said more than once." And added, in a more serious voice, "It may be I was unwise to come to Medaweska. But, as I said yesterday, I had a great desire to see again the two people who had been so kind to me years ago at Medowktek. I had no thought that my coming would arouse suspicion, and the active hostility as exemplified in M. d'Amours' outburst yesterday."

She was looking at him, her lovely eyes clouded with sorrow. "I am sorry for that, Monsieur David. I shall never cease to regret it. As for me, I know you came in amity; it was kind of you to come." She paused a moment. Then went on, her voice muted, like the soft sad flow of wind in pines at dusk, "But now, having seen us… It is unwise for you to remain longer, Monsieur David."

"You dislike me?" he asked, a pain in his words. "Oh no!" she answered hastily, "I do not dislike you, Monsieur David."

Impulsively he put out a hand and laid it over hers clasped in her lap.

For a brief moment she allowed him to imprison it, then quietly withdrew it.

"That is why I came this afternoon. To say you *must* go." She glanced fearfully about her, then continued, "You do not realize what danger you run by staying longer."

He said, "Is it Etienne who may do me injury?"

"Yes, yes, Monsieur. You do not know him. He hates all English and Scots."

"Did Monsieur d'Amours go on a hunt to-day?" he asked.

"Yes, Monsieur. He left this morning; said he would be gone until nightfall. But—" again she paused, then continued, "He hates *you*, especially."

He thought he knew why Etienne d'Amours hated him. Of course the fellow was jealous.

"That is unfortunate—and, regrettable, Mademoiselle. I do not enjoy having anyone, even Etienne d'Amours, hate me."

"Yes, Monsieur David, I can understand how you feel about it. And believe me, I would not have told you what has given you pain, were it not necessary to impress upon you the danger you run."

"You are all that is generous, and I thank you," he said earnestly, smiling down at her upturned face. "You too, are persistent, Mademoiselle Jeanne."

She nodded gravely.

He went on, "I do not fear Etienne, Mademoiselle; and therefore I shall not leave until—"

"Oh," she cried, "you do not understand! Let me explain: If any ill were to happen to you, if you failed to return to the Fort, soldiers would come to investigate. It would mean our ruin. Do you now comprehend, Monsieur David?"

For a moment he thought she was concerned only for her own people, but, sweeping it aside as unworthy, he said:

"Pardon me, Mademoiselle, if I ask a very personal question: Are you promised to wed Etienne d'Amours?"

"No, no, Monsieur David," she answered quickly.

He gave a sigh of relief, "Or any one else?" he pursued.

She made no immediate reply. He loved her. She had known it yesterday. What he had said then, as well as now, was as revealing as any formal declaration he might make. Yet because she too loved, and even though she was convinced in her mind they must part— because of Etienne, as well as for other reasons—she wanted to hear his voice say what she feared to hear. She realized she was weaker than she had thought.

The fact that she loved had come to her last night, lying awake in her bunk. It had swept over her with such force her heart pounded in her throat and she had felt breathless. Getting up, she had put on her skirt, slipped her feet into her moccasins, and had gone out into the starlit night. Walking over to the great pine tree—the earth beneath it carpeted with needles and cones dropped throughout the long years—and leaning her back against its trunk, she had stood there with closed eyes, her hands interlocked across her breasts, while the discovery of her love swept through her like a pain; like a joyous pain. She had waited a long time for love to enter her life, and, now that it had come, she knew not what to do with it. There were so many issues at stake—obstacles that seemed for the moment insurmountable.

His face was close to hers, "You have not answered my question, Mademoiselle Jeanne."

She gave a low sigh. "I am not promised to wed any one," she said slowly; and started to get up from the log. But he put a hand on her arm and gently detained her.

"Please," he said, "do not go yet; there is so much more I would say."

She gazed up at him, a whimsical look in her eyes. "But we do not get anywhere, Monsieur David. Our talk is like a squirrel in a cage. It travels always back to the place it started from." She ended with a little nervous laugh, knowing she was again on dangerous ground.

"Listen, Mademoiselle Jeanne," he said earnestly, "you have told me you do not love any one. And—"

"Oh," she interjected quickly, "I did not say *that*. Because one can love, and not be promised to wed. Is it not so, Monsieur David?"

"Yes, of course," he answered, with a crestfallen look. After a short pause, "I had hoped you did not love any one, Mademoiselle Jeanne."

She looked away. She had not intended the conversation should take this course. It was like setting little wood chips adrift on a current. Once started, one never knew what turns they would make, or whither go. Her heart recklessly said to herself: "Let it go on." Her head: "This play of words must cease." For she knew beyond all doubt, that were he to declare his love, her will to refuse him would be weakened.

What mattered? Love was everything. Others besides Etienne had asked her hand in marriage. But she had said them nay. Now that love had come, was she to put it from her? Her brain worked quickly. She would have a talk with her father, tell him everything, make plans to leave while Etienne was away on a hunt. He would go tomorrow, as usual. Once in Tomah's canoe, the Chief would be far beyond pursuit before his return.

So finally she turned and met David's eyes, her own filled with tender light, and said, her voice low, vibrant with feeling.

"But I do, Monsieur David." And thought: Now will he say what is in his heart?

She waited expectantly for his answer, during which the very air was vibrant with her knowledge of his undeclared love. In her state of exaltation all thought of Etienne, her duty to her father, were non-existent. No more was she conscious of the sibilant sound of the waterfall, or of air, or of trees, or of sunlight. Then, as his voice broke on the silence, she realized that her heart was thumping wildly, and as though it were confined in too small a space.

"Oh," he said dejectedly, "perhaps one of the officers of Boishébert's garrison, when he was at Fort Nerepis? Or some one you met at Quebec? There were many eligible men there."

She raised her hand in a little helpless gesture. He was so stupid not to know the truth! She had a quick desire to shake him gently. "I shall not say so, Monsieur David. Yes, I shall: It is *not* an officer who was of Boishébert's garrison; nor one I met at Quebec." And she thought: Now he can go on.

He said in a low voice half choked with emotion, "Oh, well, all I can say is that the fellow you love must be blind."

For a few moments she was too dumbfounded to reply. He was impossible! She was sorry for him, sorry for herself. Finally, with an assumption of indifference she nowise felt, she said lightly:

"Yes, that is *my* thought too. But many men are like that. I…" She paused, finger upraised, as a hidden bird unloosed its flawless notes from a nearby thicket. "You hear it?" she asked, her voice barely audible.

"Yes," he answered. "It is the song sparrow. Hark—there it is again."

When the notes had ended he said to her, "It is singing: *Ti-ne-li-ain-Nicolai-Nicolai-Denys-Denys*? That, Mademoiselle Jeanne, is how the Micmac Indians render the song. Let me explain: One day, while I was a prisoner of the Maliseets at Medowktek, before Tomah returned, and set me free, some Micmac warriors came to the village on their way to make war on the New Englanders.

"As they sat in front of the big Council Lodge, a song sparrow sang from a thicket of alders near the river bank. And one of the Micmacs said, 'That is Nicolas Denys' little bird. Nicolas Denys he lived a long time ago, at Chedabuctu, in Micmac country. He had a big fort and truck house. Always he travel in the woods, where Micmacs have wigwams, and make trade for furs. And them little birds they get to know him. So they sing: *Ti-ne-li-ain-Nicolai-Nicolai-Denys-Denys*? That means in Micmac: Where are you going, Nicolas Denys?

"'*Ah-ha*, Nicolas Denys he is dead long, long time—when my grandmother was a young squaw. But the little bird still ask where he goes. *Ah-ha*, they never tired asking him. Maybe Nicolas he hear, but can't tell.'"

David paused a moment. "It is a pretty tale, is it not, Mademoiselle?"

"Yes," she answered, her voice low with emotion. "I must remember, and tell it to my father some day." And in a flash she realized that she could not go away and leave him. He had been to her both father and mother these many years—years in which they had shared the almost daily fear that the English would come and, overpowering them, send them into exile. He was no longer young. Were she to leave him, who would care for him in his old age, or in sickness? She had been momentarily mad to think of seizing personal happiness at the expense of his well-being. Yes, she must put an end to this enchanting hour—even though she felt her heart to be breaking.

Resolutely she got to her feet, picked up her gun, then, turning to David, who had also risen, pained surprise on his face: "I am sorry, my friend, I…" She paused. There was a choking sensation in her throat. Bravely she held back the tears, and, ignoring his outstretched hand, continued, "I must go. Do you go also, David. It is my wish, please. And may the Saints bless you. Adieu." She almost ran along the path away from him.

He called her name. But if she heard she did not turn, and in a few moments was lost to view.

22

He sank down on the fallen log, chin cupped in his hands, a dull pain in his heart, while he gazed ruefully at the ground.

Suddenly the song sparrow began again: "*Ti-ne-li-ain-Nicolai…*" Then ceased, its theme unfinished.

The Scot smiled sadly, and, now conscious of the presence of some one, he looked up hopefully—thinking it might be Jeanne—to see Etienne d'Amours gazing down at him, his dark eyes somber and menacing.

David was the first to speak. "Ah," he said, "it is you, Monsieur?" And got quickly to his feet.

"Yes, it is I, Etienne d'Amours," announced the Acadian coldly. "You have not gone, Monsieur Cameron. It is time."

"And who gave you the right to say so, M'sieu?" asked David, roused to quick anger, as well by the Acadian's insulting manner, as by the suspicion that he had heard at least some of the conversation between him and Jeanne Chartier.

D'Amours spoke with heat: "It is *my* right, Monsieur. It is my right to protect my people of Medaweska, who will now be happy to see the last of you."

"Did the good people of Medaweska make you their deputy?" asked David calmly.

"Monsieur Cameron has not the right to question me," said d'Amours. "Monsieur was not asked to come. It is Etienne d'Amours who is telling him to go!" He paused a moment. "And let me tell you this, Monsieur: Some day this country will again be French. Then we will cut the throat of every Englishman, and every Scot!"

There comes the time when even the most peaceful-minded person feels that he has taken enough insults. David had now reached that stage. And there was a dangerous glint in his eyes, as, lapsing into English, all forgetful at the moment that d'Amours did not know the language, he said quickly, with his broad Scots accent:

"It would take a heap of cutting, Monsieur. The worrld has been trying to do the job for a good many hundred years, especially Scots' throats—and we are still carrying on the breed."

"Will Monsieur speak French, or Indian?" snapped d'Amours. Then added, "Although Monsieur's French is bad enough!"

"Aye," said David. "And I crave your pardon for using my mother tongue. I will say this, Monsieur: I will remain the night with Tomah, see Monsieur Chartier in the morning, transact my business with him; after which, if both he and Mademoiselle ask me to depart, I will do so; not one moment before. Now, Monsieur d'Amours, you have my answer."

D'Amours' eyes blazed with hate. He flung up his gun, then, with a curse, stood it against the trunk of a tree, and turning on David, cried:

"I will kill you with my hands, Monsieur, because it would be a waste of good powder and ball to shoot you. Prepare, Monsieur!"

He was upon David with the fury of an angry bear.

The Scot was hurled backwards, but managed to grasp his assailant by the wrists. "Back, d'Amours!" he cried. "Back, I say!"

He might as well have appealed to a thunderbolt to change its course. With a sudden wrench d'Amours broke David's hold on his wrists, and drove his clenched fist into his face with such force David was sent staggering backwards. Again d'Amours was upon him, swinging his arms like flails.

David stepped quickly to right and left in his efforts to evade the fellow's mad charges. Again he appealed to d'Amours to cease. Then, realizing that he must fight, he warded off a blow meant for his face, and brought his right fist upwards to d'Amours' chin with such force it sent him to his knees, where he stayed half stupefied, gazing up with glassy eyes at the Scot.

David spoke. "I am sorry, d'Amours; more than sorry that this has happened. Come, I bear you no ill-will." He held out his hand. "You have fought a bonny fight, and I would not do you more injury. Come, M'sieu, I would part in friendship. Let me help you up."

Ignoring the proffered hand, the Acadian got slowly to his feet, took a few steps away, turned with the agility of a panther, leaped into the air, and with both feet struck David a blow on the chest that stretched him flat on the turf. Now he threw himself upon his prostrate foe, beating at his face with his fists; in his rage intent on killing this foreigner who had dared to make love to the woman he himself had failed to win.

He rained blow after blow. With fiendish joy he saw the blood spurt from the pallid brow of his enemy. He grasped him by the throat and shook him with all his strength.

Suddenly he heard a rock crash down the bank into the brook, and glancing in that direction saw Tomah clambering up the incline, towards him.

Etienne sprang to his feet; darted to the tree where he had stood his gun; seized it and vanished into the woods.

Tomah laid his gun on the sward, dropped to his knees beside David, felt his wrist, put his ear to his chest. Then, picking up David's hat, he ran to the brook and dipped it full with water. Back again, he dashed some into David's face, splashed some on his wrists.

It seemed to Tomah ages before David gave a low sigh, opened his eyes, and gazed dully up at his face. Slowly he felt his bruised lips with his tongue, gave another sigh. "Oh," he muttered, "what has happened, Tomah?"

Tomah did not answer. He again picked up David's hat, slid down the bank and refilled it. Back again, he knelt and held it to David's mouth. "Drink, P'sazum," he said.

David gulped greedily, the water pouring off his chin to his neck. "Ah," he whispered, "that is *Ka-loo-ut* (good), Tomah."

"*Ah-ha*," said Tomah. "My son is now better?"

"Yes. Please lift me up, Tomah."

So Tomah put an arm under his shoulders and raised him to a sitting posture.

David put a hand to his brow, felt his bruised face. He said thickly, "The fellow gave me a frightful beating. I can sit alone, now, Tomah, thank you." He felt in his pocket for his handkerchief and drew it out. "Will you wet it, Tomah?" he asked. "I am afraid my face is rather a mess."

Tomah poured the remaining water from the hat on the handkerchief, and tenderly washed the blood from David's face. This done, he walked over, picked up his gun, looked at the pan, renewed the priming, and, a determined look on his face, was starting off when David said,

"Where are you going, my father?"

The Chief turned, looked down into David's eyes and announced grimly, "Tomah goes on the *ski-dup-way* (man's) trail."

"No—no, my father!" cried David. "I say *no*. Come, do not leave me. I…I need more water."

Never in all their years of comradeship had he spoken so peremptorily to the Chief. Slowly Tomah laid his gun on the ground. "It will be as my son says," he said quietly. And going to the brook with David's hat returned and gave him another drink.

"*Wul-e-wun* (thank you), my father," said David.

Reaching out he laid his hand gently on the Chief's. "Why did you come up the brook, my father?"

"I knew my son was in danger. I came quick. Tomah is *Me-ta-o-lin*," announced the Chief.

"Ah," said David, knowing that the word meant one who was able to foresee events, as well as to work magic. Then he added, "P'sazum loves his father. He is thankful. Now, Tomah, help me up, please. I will go back to the wigwam."

But when he stood, and took a deep breath, he clapped a hand to his side and gave an exclamation of pain.

"My son, are you *k's-en-ok* (in pain)?" asked Tomah anxiously.

"A little," answered David. "But I'm all right; I can go now."

So with Tomah carrying both guns under his right arm, and with his left supporting David, they slowly retraced their steps to the little wigwam by the brookside.

Here the Scot lay down. He asked for his little mirror, which Tomah brought to him. Ruefully he surveyed his bruised and swollen face. "I'm a pretty sight!" he muttered to himself, handing Tomah back the mirror.

His head ached from its terrific impact when it had struck the ground. Moreover, he feared that some of his ribs had been fractured when d'Amours had kicked him. But Tomah, after he had bared the upper part of his body, and felt about with his fingers, said:

"Ribs they not broke, my son." Nevertheless, he took David's plaid, and carefully folding it to a wide band, he bound it firmly about the injured part. It made David feel more at ease, though he still suffered when he took a deep breath; which fact caused him to think that the Chief's diagnosis was at fault. However, he needed no assurance that he had taken a sad if treacherous defeat at the hands of d'Amours. Doubtless the fellow had killed him but for Tomah's timely arrival.

He slept little that night. He suffered both physically and mentally. The woman he had come hoping to wed had frankly admitted she loved, and, though not promised to wed, had plainly told him it was her wish that he leave Medaweska. At the last she had seemed greatly perturbed, almost hysterical. That was natural. For she knew, as well as he did, that if d'Amours were to injure him fatally, those at the fort would soon know and inflict on the Acadians death or exile.

Ruefully he told himself that no woman of Jeanne Chartier's quick intelligence could fail to grasp the fact that he was in love with her. She had been kind to him, not wishing to hurt by allowing him to confess in so many words an attachment she could not return.

And yet, in confessing that she loved, she had not spoken like one heart-broken. On the contrary, she had been quite casual about it—yes, a little flippant; as though it were a fact that must be accepted, and it would do no possible good to continue mourning over what could not be helped.

Well, all that was left for him now was to go up to the settlement on the morrow, or the following day, see Monsieur Chartier, explain his proposition for the establishing of truck houses on the river; and, after a final farewell to Jeanne, return to Medowktek; stay there a few days, then go down to the harbour and rejoin his ship.

23

But, on the morrow, the Scot was unable to move from the wigwam. He ached in every muscle, and told himself he was running a fever. Tomah brought him water to drink, and otherwise cared for his every need.

The Chief more than once spoke of d'Amours, calling him that *mu-jeg'n ski-dup* (bad man); adding that he would like to take his scalp. He kept his gun loaded and the pan primed, and spent some of his spare time whetting his long knife. Which noting, David told him that if he were to do any injury to the fellow it would grieve him exceedingly. The Indian listened respectfully, finally said:

"Might be my son is wise. But if Tomah has an enemy, he kills him. P'sazum's enemy is Tomah's enemy."

"No, my father. There will be no killing! Promise me, Tomah," he insisted.

The Chief was silent a few moments, then said slowly, "*Ah-ha*, if the *ski-dup* does not come again to harm him it will be as my son says. But if the *ski-dup* comes to kill, Tomah will kill."

He said it with such firm resolve that David knew it was futile to argue further with him at present.

24

The days passed. At the end of the week, save for the unhealed scar on his forehead, David was wholly recovered and ready to travel. He had written three letters: one to Colonel Arbuthnot, the second to Captain Fortescue, and the third to his partner, Ian Grahme.

And, for the reason that, should d'Amours succeed in doing him fatal injury, all the people of Medaweska, and of the whole river of the Maliseets would surely suffer, he wrote in such a manner that the English commander would be convinced his death was entirely an accident.

To Colonel Arbuthnot he said in part: I have had an unfortunate accident from which I cannot recover. It all comes of being careless with firearms. You will receive this note by the hands of Chief Tomah. I much regret that I shall be unable to thank you in person for your courtesy in helping me secure the services of the two Indians who brought me up the river. They were most satisfactory. Nor did any member of the tribe offer me harm whatsoever. From my knowledge of them, a wise and generous policy will do more to win their loyalty and regard than the use of force. As for the few Acadians remaining on the river, I sincerely trust that eventually the instincts of humanity will cause the victors to observe towards them that spirit of charity and love enjoined upon mankind by our Heavenly Father.

With which, my dear Sir, I subscribe myself.

    Most faithfully yours,

    David Malcolm Cameron

Saint John River,

September 15th, 1761.

To Captain Fortescue he merely repeated that he had received an accidental wound from which he could not recover. He was to take the *Sheila Grahme* back to Aberdeen, and deliver the enclosed letter to his partner, who would more carefully acquaint him with the facts of the case. He instructed the captain to give Tomah all the food from the ship's stores his canoe would hold; also plenty of powder, ball, and extra flints for his gun.

His letter to Ian was more particular as to the probable cause of his "accident." Then he briefly unfolded his plan for truck houses.

If his partner agreed, it would first be necessary to consult with the Secretary of State, and petition him to grant the right to engage in private trade on the Saint John and other waters. If this were granted, one of the smaller vessels of the firm, loaded with supplies for truck, should sail in the spring to the River Saint John, and go up to St. Ann's. Her captain was then to engage an Indian at Ek-pa-hawk to take him by canoe to Medowktek, where he would meet Chief Tomah, who would conduct him to Medaweska. Here the captain was to confer with Monsieur Raoul Chartier, who knew about the project.

In any case, whether Ian fell in with his plan or not, it was his will that five hundred pounds in gold be transported yearly to the Saint John River in Acadia, and placed in the hands of Mademoiselle Jeanne Chartier, daughter of Monsieur Raoul Chartier, at the mouth of the Medaweska River; or, if she had changed her place of residence, whithersoever she might be, for the term of her natural life, single, or married.

And he added: "This, my dear friend, is a solemn trust I repose in you, whom I have loved from boyhood as a brother."

Then, having addressed his letter to Colonel Arbuthnot, he enclosed those to Captain Fortescue and Ian Grahme in birch bark, and bound the package with a withe of the same material. Now he sat down opposite Tomah and said:

"My father, if anything should happen to me, and I should die, it is my wish that you take these two letters to the mouth of the river: This one," and he held up his letter to Colonel Arbuthnot, "is to be given into the hands of the commander of the Fort. And this," holding up the package containing those to Captain Fortescue and

Ian Grahme, "is to be given into the hands of Captain Fortescue, who is in command of my ship. If the ship has not arrived, you will wait there until she does. Do you understand, my father?"

"*Ah-ha*," said Tomah. "But I do not understand why my son…" He paused a moment. Then, a hard look in his eyes, he went on, "Does my son mean that the *ski-dup* might kill him?"

"Yes, that is what I mean, my father. And to any questions they may ask you concerning the cause of my death, you are only to say, "It is *all* in the letter."

And, having said this to Tomah, he knew that neither beguilement, nor torture, nor fear of death, would wring from the Chief one word more than he had told him to say.

Then said Tomah, "After I have killed the *ski-dup*, I will go to the mouth of the river, and give the letter to Colonel Arbuthnot, and the captain of my son's ship."

For half an hour David argued with the Chief in his efforts to convince him that no matter what happened, he was not to take the life of d'Amours. Finally, Tomah threw himself face down on the sand, making no movement for several minutes. At last he rose slowly to his feet, and looking down at David, said sadly:

"I have talked with the Great Spirit. It will be as my son says." And without another word he walked down to the beach, lifted up his canoe, brought it near the fire, and heating pitch mixed with ashes, he carefully spread it over any of the seams that showed signs of cracking.

While he was still working, a Maliseet Indian and his squaw who had been on a hunt farther up the river, and were now returning to Medowktek, came opposite them. Recognizing Tomah, the hunter swung his canoe close to shore and spoke to him. He told the Chief that several people in the Acadian settlement were sick with the plague. A Frenchman who had been on a hunt to the northward had been taken with it, and had just time to stagger into the village when he fell in a faint. Now others were sick. The white chief, Monsieur Chartier, was very bad, and his daughter feared he might die. The Indian described the onset of the disease: a heavy cold, with bleeding at the nose, then pain in the chest, and a bad cough. He advised Tomah to flee down river as he was doing.

From the Maliseet's description, David was of the opinion that the disease was a virulent type of influenza, such as on several occasions in times past had devastated the aborigines of New England and the Saint John River.

When they had departed, he told Tomah that he would go at once to the settlement and do what he could to aid the stricken people. And added, "I have medicines with me, my father, and know how to use them."

The Chief tried to dissuade him, telling him that he too might take the sickness. But although David thanked him for his solicitude for his welfare, he said he was determined to go. He added, "Do you take me up to the village, my father, put me on shore, then you come back here and wait for me."

The Chief gave a low laugh. "You stay—Tomah will stay too," he announced with quiet finality.

25

And so it was that after loading the baggage in the canoe, they embarked, and Tomah poled up to the mouth of the Medaweska.

Landing, David went at once to the cabin of Raoul Chartier. Jeanne came to the door. She was pale and hollow-eyed. She betrayed no surprise at seeing him.

"I was told you had not gone, Monsieur." And added, "My father is seriously ill, as are several others in the settlement. One has died. A courier has been sent to the Rivière du Loup to get the priest, if he is there. He has a knowledge of medicine." She paused, searched his face quickly, and added, "You have been injured, Monsieur?"

He smiled. "It is nothing, Mademoiselle. I had a fall some days ago." Then, "I too, have a knowledge of medicine. True, it is small, but I may be of some help."

"It is not right for Monsieur to remain here. You may take the plague. Besides, the priest will come in a day or two."

"I am staying," announced David. "Surely, even though I am hated in this place, you will not refuse my proffered assistance."

She looked at him, her eyes troubled, but made no reply. She stepped to one side, and he entered the cabin. Monsieur Chartier was lying on his bunk, eyes closed, face flushed. As David approached he muttered disjointed phrases in French and Maliseet.

David bent and felt his brow. It was as hot as fire. The sick man opened his eyes, stared up at David and said:

"It is you, Etienne?" and began coughing. It racked his whole body.

Said Jeanne:

"He has been like this for two days. Sometimes he knows not even me."

David turned, went to the door and called Tomah:

"My father," he said, "do you go and get some of the roots of the pond-lily."

Without a word the Chief departed. David took out his small medicine box, that among other things contained senna leaves and quinine. He asked Jeanne for warm water and a spoon. She brought both. He took the spoon, half filled it with water, and dropped in a sufficient dose of the quinine powder. When it was dissolved, he turned to the sick man, roused him, and, a supporting arm beneath his shoulders, raised him slightly, and put the spoon to his lips.

Monsieur Chartier swallowed with difficulty, then whispered hoarsely, "Thank you, Etienne."

The Scot allowed him to sink back on the pillow. Taking out his watch, he looked at the time and said to Jeanne:

"In two hours we must give him more. In a little while we will give him some senna tea."§

She made no reply save, "Thank you, Monsieur. You are very kind."

He smiled. "I pray you not to worry, Mademoiselle. I am quite sure the medicine will make him well." He went to the fireplace, beside which some wood was piled, and replenished the fire. Then he added, "When Tomah comes back I will give medicine to the others who are sick, if you will show me their cabins."

"Yes, Monsieur."

"Is Monsieur d'Amours in the village?" he asked.

"Not at present, Monsieur. He is gone to hunt. It may be he will return by nightfall." She ceased, went to her father, and sitting down on a small wooden bench, took out a string of beads with its crucifix from her skirt pocket, and slowly fingered them one by one, her lips moving silently.

David drew a stool to the fireplace and sat down. He took out his pipe, held it in his hand a few moments, returned it to his pocket. He glanced at the bent head of the girl. Her lips still moved in soundless prayer; often the fingers telling the beads hesitated and trembled a moment, then resolutely continued.

His heart ached for her. He would have given anything to be able to comfort her. He knew that Monsieur Chartier was a very sick man. He thought there might be a slight congestion of the lungs, but hoped to break it up with quinine and poultices. What would happen to Jeanne; to whom would she go, did her remaining parent die? Of course there were the relatives in Quebec. But would she want to leave her Acadian people?

He wondered why some of the womenfolk had not come to help her; answered his own mental thought by telling himself they were too afraid of the plague to enter the cabin. Later, he found such was the case.

Now he gave Monsieur Chartier senna tea, and, when the two hours had passed since the first dose of quinine, he asked Jeanne for more warm water. She rose and brought it.

He took the spoon, put into it a little of the water, then the quinine, and stirred it; when it was dissolved, he again lifted the shoulders of the sick man.

"More medicine, Monsieur," he said.

Monsieur Chartier parted his lips. As he swallowed the bitter stuff he made a wry face, but said nothing. David eased his head back on the pillow.

The girl spoke, "What is the nature of the powder, Monsieur?"

"It is quinine," he answered. "It has been used for more than a hundred years, not only in Europe, but by your Jesuit priests in America. It induces sweat, allays fever. I feel quite sure it will make him well."

"Thank you, Monsieur," she said simply.

He thought to himself: She has not once called me "monsieur David"; only "monsieur". She was speaking:

"I shall prepare you something to eat, Monsieur—not much, for food is even scarcer in the village. That is why Etienne went into the forest today, hoping to shoot a moose, or deer. We would be glad even to have bear meat."

"Oh," he said, "I have some fish—trout that Tomah took this morning at the mouth of the brook. I had quite forgotten. I will go to the canoe and get them."

He went out and down to the river where Tomah had turned the canoe bottom-up on the beach. Reaching underneath it he took out the trout, wrapped in moss and birch bark, then his canister of tea and the small copper kettle.

Going back, he saw one of the Acadians standing dejectedly outside the door of his cabin. His eyes were red and swollen, as though he had been weeping. Approaching him, David said, "Have you sick people in your house, Monsieur?"

"My wife, M'sieu. My son, the eldest, died a few minutes ago. God be with us." And the Acadian crossed himself.

"I am sorry," said David. Then added, "I have medicine. In a little while I will come and give some of it to your wife."

"Thank you, Monsieur."

26

Entering Monsieur Chartier's cabin, David found that Jeanne had set pewter plates and mugs on the table. On each plate was a thick round of corn bread; a cup held maple syrup. There was also a small jug of milk.

Resting on the crane in the fireplace was an iron skillet into which the girl had put water to boil.

David removed three of the trout from the birch bark box. They were fat; fully a pound in weight.

"One for you, one for me, and one for Tomah," he said. Then holding up the canister: "I also have some China tea, Mademoiselle."

She smiled. "We had it occasionally, at the governor's palace. But mostly, when not wine, our drink was coffee. I believe tea is more used by the English than by our French, is it not so, Monsieur?"

"Yes, Mademoiselle, but we use coffee also; perhaps one as much as the other. In the mid-sixteenth century it was called China drink. My partner and I have imported many thousands of pounds of the leaves to England. Will you have a cup, Mademoiselle, if I brew some?"

"Certainly, Monsieur, and thank you." She took the fish from his hands and put them into the skillet. Then she said, "I am sorry we have so little food—Monsieur is not used to such poverty at his home."

"It does not matter about my home," he said. "It is a long distance away. And I have known poverty, Mademoiselle, and hunger; as when Tomah and I travelled from Virginia through the forest. And later, at Medowktek, some times we feasted, or again we went hungry until moose or fish were taken. And so, Mademoiselle, it is a privilege to eat again at your table, and

I thank you. Have you fresh water, Mademoiselle? Because it needs fresh water to make tea."

"I will get some, Monsieur," and she started towards the bench by the door on which stood two birch bark buckets.

"Allow *me*, Mademoiselle," he said. But she shook her head. "No, Monsieur does not know the path to the spring, which is in the woods. It is not far. Will you please to watch my father until I return?"

"Yes, Mademoiselle. But you must later show me where the spring is so that I can fetch water for you."

When she had gone he went over to Monsieur Chartier and touched his brow. It was still hot and dry. He felt the pulse. Its beat was hurried.

The door opened. It was Tomah. He carried a bundle of lily roots, each as big as plantain stocks. He said, "Tomah went to the dead water above the falls. Plenty roots there. I cut poles, made a raft. Hard time to get them. Moose not been in the dead water for a long time. See track of bear, three, four days old."

Jeanne entered, put her bucket of water on a bench below the small window, spoke to Tomah, then poured some into David's copper kettle and set it to boil.

Monsieur Chartier began coughing. It racked his whole body. The girl ran on moccasined feet to his side, raised him a little until the paroxysm had ceased; eased him gently back. Then, feeling his brow, she looked up at David, her eyes troubled, and said, "It is still hot—too hot, Monsieur."

He said soothingly, "That is natural, Mademoiselle. But when he has had more quinine, I am sure the fever will go down."

She smiled wanly. "You are comforting, Monsieur."

The meal over, David told Tomah to crush one of the lily stalks with the pole of his axe. When it was reduced to an oily mass, David explained to Jeanne it was for a poultice, and he needed a piece of cotton or woollen cloth, preferably woollen.

She nodded. Going to a wooden chest she opened it and brought back to him a woollen shirt of her father's. Laying it on the table, David put in the crushed lily root, folded the edges of the shirt over it, and placed the flattened bundle on one of the hot stones in the fireplace. He said to the girl, "It is an old Indian remedy for congestion of the chest I learned from the Maliseet women. Would you have oil of any kind, Mademoiselle?"

"But yes, Monsieur," she answered eagerly. She went to a little shelf to one side of the fireplace, lifted down a bottle, and coming back, said, "Etienne uses it to make scent for his traps."

"I shall need only a little," he said. Lifting up the poultice, he placed the unheated side on the hot stone. He turned to the girl. "The poultice will soon be ready, Mademoiselle. Will you now rub a little of the oil on your father's chest?"

She did his bidding.

A few minutes later he lifted up the poultice, bared his own wrist, pressed it against the heated mass, then, with a satisfied nod, "It is hot, but it will not burn." Going over, he placed the poultice on Chartier's chest, covered it with the blankets, and turned to the girl. "Tomah will now watch," he said. "Will you kindly show me the cabins where the other sick people are?"

"You are so good to help us. I can never thank you enough, Monsieur David. Yes, come—I will show you where the sick are."

A thrill of delight passed over him that she had again called him by his given name. He picked up the little box containing his precious medicines and followed her out of the cabin.

27

An hour later he returned, having given senna and quinine to a dozen of the stricken people.

He found that Tomah had brought his canoe from the river and placed it bottom-up beneath the big pine tree. He had cut two forked poles about five feet long and placed the ends into the ground, with the forked ends engaging the gunwale. Beneath it he had made a long bed of soft fir boughs upon which he spread their blankets.

He said, "*Wul-e-na-gwit* wigwam, P'sazum." (It is a nice looking wigwam.)

"*Ka-loo-ut* (good)," agreed David. He went into the cabin, found Etienne d'Amours seated on a stool gazing moodily into the fireplace. He looked up, and seeing David, his face flushed a dark red. He rose quickly to his feet.

The Scot was the first to speak. "Good afternoon, Monsieur," he said cordially.

The Acadian inclined his head in a slight bow.

"Mademoiselle Chartier tells me you have been doing the good work."

"Oh," said David, "I had some few medicines which providentially I knew how to use. I am thinking that Monsieur Chartier will soon improve." He turned to Jeanne, "Have you again heated the poultice, Mademoiselle?" he asked.

"But a little while ago, Monsieur. I had Tomah make me another, so that when one is cooled, we shall have a hot one to put on."

"That is wise," he remarked. "We must keep it up all night to increase the flow of blood to the chest." He turned to d'Amours, "Did Monsieur find moose?"

"Nothing but a partridge and a rabbit," answered the Acadian morosely. "François Robechaud and I travelled all day. But we saw nothing. We will go again tomorrow." He sat down and began to fill his pipe.

"I will ask Tomah to go with you tomorrow—or in another direction," said David.

D'Amours made no comment. He merely nodded his head, then lighted his pipe with a brand from the fireplace.

Jeanne got up from the stool beside her father's bunk, and said to d'Amours, "I will get you some food, Etienne. I have some trout and tea Monsieur Cameron brought."

For a few moments d'Amours made no comment. Then, "I have not much hunger, Jeanne. I will eat a corn bread, and the slice of cold meat I did not use today. It is enough."

The suspicion that d'Amours wanted none of his trout or tea shocked David. He looked at his watch. He waited until Jeanne had set the table for d'Amours, then told her it was time for more medicine.

When it had been given he went outside. Darkness was falling. He found that Tomah had made a little fire in front of the upturned canoe. He was smoking his pipe and staring into the flames. He looked up:

"The *ski-dup* (man) has come back."

"Yes," said David, knowing he meant d'Amours.

"*Mut-geg'n n'ski-dup*" (very bad man)," announced Tomah. "My son must watch him."

"Oh, he will not harm me now. You see, my father, I am now medicine man." And going to the row of Acadian cabins which housed the sick he visited one after another, and administered more quinine.

28

It was long after dark when he returned to Monsieur Chartier's cabin. There was no light save that given off by the logs in the fireplace. Only dimly could he make out the form of the girl seated beside her father, who was again delirious. D'Amours had gone to his own little cabin a few rods distant. David was glad. Although he was sure the fellow would not now provoke a quarrel. his continued presence in the cabin would have been embarrassing to both.

He went over to Jeanne. "We will now give him one more dose of quinine, Mademoiselle. Then no more until morning."

She rose, got warm water, the cup and spoon, and came back to him. When they had given him the medicine, he said to her, "Do you lie down Mademoiselle. I shall watch and renew the poultices."

When she demurred, he insisted gently, "You have had no sleep for several nights, Mademoiselle Jeanne. It is better to rest so that you can carry on tomorrow. Besides, when one is exhausted, it is easier to get the disease. And so, please go to sleep, and fear not. I will keep awake and do all that is necessary."

She rose wearily. "Perhaps it is better so, Monsieur David." She paused a moment, then, "I think the good God has sent you. I shall say a little prayer for you, Monsieur David."

He wanted to reach out, take her in his arms and comfort her with loving words. Instead, he said softly, "I shall always remember that you have prayed for me, Mademoiselle." He saw that she was swaying on her feet with weariness, and added:

"Go now, please, Mademoiselle Jeanne."

She walked over to her bunk against the farther wall, and sinking to her knees, her eyes on the crucifix, said her prayer. Then she laid herself down on her bunk.

A moment later he heard her low voice, "If he gets worse, Monsieur, you will call me at once?"

"Yes," he said, "do not worry, Mademoiselle Jeanne."

After putting more logs on the fire he seated himself beside the sick man.

29

The hours passed. He could hear the gentle breathing of the girl, and knew she was sound asleep. At intervals he put another poultice on Monsieur Chartier's chest. There was no sound save the flickering of the flames up the broad stone chimney, occasionally the mumbled words of the sick man in his delirium.

Often David found himself dozing. Then he would shake his head to rouse himself. He *must not* lose consciousness. He had promised to keep awake. Finally he filled his pipe, got it lighted and again sat down on his bench.

When the pipe was empty, he looked at his watch. Only midnight! He repressed a yawn, got up, and searching in his pack he took out his well thumbed copy of *Pilgrim's Progress.*

Again seated, he read as best he could by the feeble light the beautiful allegory of Christian's adventures in his efforts to find the Celestial City.

He read on and on until, finally, the text floated before his eyes. He stifled another yawn, rose, and going to the fireplace heated another poultice. As he returned to the bunk he stumbled, regained his balance with great effort, and heard Monsieur Chartier's voice.

"Is that you, Jeanne?"

She was on her feet in an instant, glided to his bunk and knelt beside him. "Yes, yes," she cried, "it is Jeanne!"

She bent and kissed his brow. Then, with a little cry of gladness, she turned to David, "His brow is moist, Monsieur." And began to weep.

David reached down and felt Monsieur Chartier's face. "Yes, Mademoiselle," he said, "the fever has turned."

Monsieur Chartier was speaking, concern in his voice. "Are you weeping, Jeanne?"

"A little, father," she answered. "But it is from happiness."

"Ah…it is good to be happy… Was it yesterday I became sick?"

"It is four days, father."

"Four days!" he repeated. "It does not seem that long. I have had bad dreams. I thought a great bear had killed our little cow. Then that the English had come, and told us we must go to the commandant at the fort… Is that Etienne back of you, Jeanne?"

"No, father," she said hurriedly, "it is Monsieur Cameron. He came yesterday. He gave you the medicine: it was the good quinine the Fathers use for sickness. Monsieur Cameron has also ministered to the other sick people. He has indeed been our good angel."

Monsieur Chartier spoke, "I thank you, Monsieur. You have been most kind." He added, "I will sleep now, Jeanne; but first I should like to have a drink of water."

They gave him the water, and in a few moments he was asleep.

Jeanne looked up at David. "I have had sleep; now I will stay awake and renew the poultices. Do you lie down and rest, Monsieur David, on my bed."

"Thank you, Mademoiselle Jeanne, but I shall sleep with Tomah, under the canoe. Tomah wakes early; and I must look after the other sick. In the meantime, if you need me, only call, and I shall hear and come." He turned to go, but she rose quickly to her feet; laying her hand on his arm, she detained him, and, her voice low, tremulous:

"If I were to live for a thousand years, Monsieur P'sazum, I could never forget what you have done, or cease to pray for you."

By the faint light from the fireplace he could see tears in her eyes. He took her small hand in his, felt it trembling, and bending his head, pressed his lips lightly to her hand. Then he walked from the room.

The September night was chill. A low mist was sweeping down the Medaweska and curling in eddies over the greater waters of the Saint John. Above the pyramidal tops of the spruces and pines that flanked the farther shore, the hunters' moon hung in solitary splendour save for one attendant star. Low in the north-east, Sirius looked like an enormous lantern suspended from the blue, inverted bowl of the sky. A flock of geese suddenly sped like a javelin far above the river, rose higher, circled with a wild clamour, then, as though their leader had decided on some more distant feeding ground, they bore north-eastward, their honks diminishing to a mere thread of sound that finally was no longer audible to the ear of the enchanted Scot.

He gave an involuntary sigh, and let his eyes rest on the drab cabins that man had laboriously set up in this far wilderness. And suddenly, from the lush grass along the shore, the bell on the neck of Antoine Cormier's cow shook out its mellow notes, incongruous with the pervading sense of native wilderness.

Beside the upturned canoe Tomah's little fire, now almost dead, gave off a small spiral of smoke. David went over, and getting to his knees, crawled beneath the birch bark canoe that had so often served them as a vehicle by day and a shelter by light. Tomah spoke:

"That you, P'sazum?"

"*Ah-ha*, my father."

"White chief better?"

"Yes," answered David. "He will now get well."

"*Ka-loo-ut* (good)," said the Chief.

With a sigh of relief David stretched himself on the fragrant bed of boughs and drew his blanket about him.

30

It seemed to him he had only been asleep a few minutes when he heard the cuffing of flint on steel, and realized that the Chief was again starting the fire. He opened his eyes, saw day had dawned. He rolled from beneath the canoe, and getting to his feet, noted that the ground was frost-covered. Tomah looked up at him. "*Ta-ka-o* (cold)," said the Chief.

David nodded. "Yes, my father." He walked down to the river; kneeling, he cupped his hands, washed, then dried himself. Now he undid the ribbon that confined his hair at the back of his neck, combed it and retied the ribbon. As he walked back to the cabin of Raoul Chartier he saw smoke coming from other chimneys of the little settlement.

He found Jeanne Chartier setting the few pewter dishes on the rude table. Etienne d'Amours was seated in front of the blazing fire, holding the long handle of a skillet into which he had put the flesh of the rabbit he had brought in last evening.

Both had turned at David's entry. The girl smiled. "Good morning, Monsieur", she said. "He is much better."

D'Amours nodded what seemed to David a reluctant greeting and again bent to his task.

The Scot went over to the bunk-side, spoke to Monsieur Chartier, took his hand, pressed his fingers to the pulse a few moments, felt the patient's brow. The pulse was about normal, the forehead moist to his touch. He smiled into Monsieur Chartier's eyes. The man smiled back, then said, "I am hungry, Monsieur. Is it right that I should have food?"

"Yes," answered David.

Jeanne had approached. "Etienne has dressed the partridge he got yesterday: it is now in the skillet boiling. We will give him broth and a little of the meat." Then to Monsieur Chartier, "It will not be long now, father."

He thanked her, and looking up at David: "Monsieur Cameron, we all owe you a debt we can never repay. As for myself, I feel a great sense of shame that we ever doubted your good intentions. Pray accept my apology, and say *you* forgive us."

"Monsieur Chartier," said David, "the little I have been privileged to do for you and your people is only a small payment for the kindness you accorded me when I was a lad at Medowktek." Then, with a gentle pressure of his hand on Monsieur Chartier's, he went to the table and seated himself.

During the breakfast Jeanne sat opposite David, Etienne to his left at one end of the table. Tomah had chosen to eat outdoors. He had mixed some of his corn meal with water, baked it on a hot stone, and had accepted a portion of the rabbit Etienne had cooked.

Etienne ate hurriedly. Any words he spoke were addressed to Jeanne. When he had finished he rose, remarking that he would find the cow and milk her.

Said Jeanne, "We will keep two pints for my father, Etienne; the rest must go to the children in the settlement."

Etienne nodded, picked up a kettle made from the bark of a birch tree, and went out, closing the door behind him.

David said to Jeanne, "How the fellow hates me!"

She held up an admonitory finger. "Sh-h," she whispered, "he has the hearing of a fox." She glanced beyond David's shoulder to the small window to the right of the door, to see d'Amours peering in at them. Quickly he withdrew his face. She heard Tomah's voice, "*Ba-kwe-nox-ne-un?*" (How do you do?) She rose, picked up a wooden spoon, went to the fireplace, and bending, stirred the partridge that was in the skillet.

David told her he was going to medicine the other sick, and getting his little box went outdoors.

The girl straightened, and, her moccasin-shod feet making no noise, crossed to the window. She saw David speak briefly to the Indian, walk quickly to the cabin of Pierre Robechaud, open the door and enter. She smiled softly to herself, then, with a sigh, went about her work.

The days passed. Each morning, and all day long at intervals, David ministered to the sick. There were no more fatalities. Raoul Chartier was now well enough to sit up in his bunk for two or three hours at a time.

One of these afternoons, while Jeanne was visiting the sick, the Scot revealed his plan to Monsieur Chartier for the establishing of truck houses on the river.

Monsieur Chartier listened attentively. When David had finished, he said:

"Monsieur Cameron, it is a good idea; but you must know that private trade is no longer permissible. All furs must now pass through the Truck Master at Fort Frederick. And so, my friend, you are beaten at the start."

David smiled. "Yes, Monsieur Chartier," he said, "I am aware of the present law regarding trucking with the Indians. But this is a decree of the governor at Halifax." He paused a moment, and went on, "I have some powerful connections in England, Monsieur Chartier, and I feel confident that after I have acquainted them with the situation in Acadia, this monopoly conferred by the governor on a few favourites will be changed."

"But even though it should be so," demurred Monsieur Chartier, "and those Acadians now on the river are allowed to remain, would any one of us be permitted to engage in trucking, that, as you have suggested, would practically control the trade of furs on the upper waters?"

"Ah," said David, "but you, Monsieur, while actually being a partner in the business, would not appear as one. You would be the company's agent, and— Pardon me, Monsieur, I know what you are about to say. But when I have conferred with the authorities in England—to whom I hold letters of introduction—I hope to be able to send you word that all the remaining Acadians on the river, from St. Ann's upwards, will be allowed to remain. This, my dear Monsieur Chartier, is one of the projects to which I am determined to devote my energy. And please forgive my conceit when I say I feel reasonably sure that my dream will become sober reality."

Then did Monsieur Chartier's eyes lighten up, and he said, "Monsieur Cameron, I cannot but be fired by your calm enthusiasm.

And whether you can bring it to pass or not, you will have my fervent thanks, as well as those of all my compatriots." He paused, his voice husky with emotion, and added, "May the good God reward you, Monsieur, for all you have done for us, as well as for your noble intentions."

31

Each day those well enough to hunt shouldered their guns and set off. Occasionally, Tomah accompanied them; but more often he went alone. Two different nights he remained in the woods by a small dead water. He had peeled a strip of white birch bark, rolled it into a cone about sixteen inches long. Putting the small end to his lips he imitated the call of the cow moose, then the raucous grunt, or bark, of the bull, in the hope of luring one of the creatures within shooting distance. It was in vain. Although the hunters covered a vast territory, they found no recent tracks made by the big animals. Rabbits and partridges were shot; and one morning, in a deadfall constructed by Paul Richard, they found a year-old bear.

A week later Father Germain, paddled by a Micmac Indian, came down the Medaweska to the little settlement. He was greeted with joy by the inhabitants. He comforted as best he could those who had lost loved ones, and said a mass for those in the new-made graves.

He explained he had been on a journey to Quebec, and had not got the message sent him to Rivière-du-Loup until his return to that place three days since.

David had not been in the village at the priest's arrival, having gone for a short walk along the beach. But when he returned, and entered Monsieur Chartier's cabin, Father Germain came forward and greeted him with outstretched hand.

"My son," he said kindly, "when years ago we parted at Medowktek, I never thought to see you again. It is the good God who sent you." He crossed himself, then went on: "I have been told by Monsieur Chartier and Mademoiselle of the good work you have done for my people. I thank you, Monsieur. I am sure God will reward you."

Thereafter Father Germain personally took over the care of the sick, though often conferring with the Scot over some particularly stubborn case.

The days, and especially the nights, had grown much colder, so the fuel problem was now almost as serious as the lack of fresh meat. David, who was a good axe-man, suggested to Father Germain that his Micmac take the place of one of the hunters, and the latter help him cut firewood.

Thus it was. Noël Cyr and David felled birch and maple trees, limbed them, then chopped them into two-foot lengths, which they later split in halves. Often the priest came and helped, his cassock tucked up to give him greater freedom of movement.

Meanwhile, the health of the remaining people in the settlement continued to improve; but the disease had been so violent, that, as in the case of Monsieur Chartier, it was to be quite long before any of them would be able to resume their ordinary tasks.

On the evening of the fifth day following the priest's coming, Tomah returned at nightfall from his day's hunt and reported he had come upon several tracks of moose heading for a snarl of ponds and dead waters, about fifteen miles north-east of the Medaweska River. It being well past midday, and as he was without food, Tomah had returned to make his report and enlist the help of other hunters.

32

The next morning three Acadians, the two Indians, and David set off in three canoes. David and Tomah were together. They poled up the Medaweska several miles until they came to a good-sized stream entering from the right, and following its course, at length entered an alder-lined brook up which they poled with difficulty for about four miles, when it suddenly opened on a fairly large pond surrounded by hills. Discarding their poles, they paddled steadily and finally entered a winding dead water, flanked on either side by a barren covered with cat-spruce, tamaracks, and shrubs of the Labrador and sheeps' laurel. The dead water was not more than a hundred yards in width. Along its shores floated roots of the lily, which Tomah told David had only recently been uprooted from the depths of the dead water by feeding moose.

He waited until the other canoes came up, when he spoke to the men. He pointed diagonally across the dead water to a leaning cedar, and told them that a canoeable brook came in from the left at that place. He suggested that D'Amours and the Micmac go up this brook a short distance; and, if they saw no moose, land and hide themselves among the shore bushes. He himself would place the others at intervals along the larger dead water. d'Amours and the Micmac agreed to this plan and immediately set off.

Then Tomah turned to David and said he would land him a few rods farther on. He now paddled the canoe to where, in the spring, a brook had wound across the barren, making a deep depression in the tundra, depositing in its journey quantities of sand and gravel from the hills from which it had its source. It was a good landing place.

When David had stepped out, Tomah explained in a low voice that, directly opposite this dried-up channel, the dead water had a hard bottom, and was a crossing place for moose and other large animals. He advised the Scot to go back along the bank a few rods, and sit down where he would have a good view along his own side of the dead water, as well as of the opposite shore. Then Tomah dipped his paddle, and followed by the remaining canoe, they both quickly sped over the mirror-like surface.

David sat down and watched them. D'Amours and his Micmac had already passed from view up the brook. Soon the other canoes swept around a point where the dead water swung sharply to the right.

He was alone. He sat with his head barely above the Labrador shrubs, his eyes alternately sweeping both sides of the barren.

Suddenly, with a whirr of wings that momentarily startled him, a flock of black ducks flew down the dead water, circled and alighted among the grass and lily pads near the opposite shore. They disturbed a muskrat, and it swam away, leaving a v-shape trail in its wake.

The ducks were close together: an easy mark, but David had had enough experience of wild life to know that even were his gun charged with small shot, the discharge of the piece would very possibly scare away any approaching moose.

A woodpecker alighted on the side of a dead tamarack a few rods distant, and hammered out his sharp, staccato notes. As though it were a challenge, the hammering was repeated from across the water. On the distant ridge a partridge drummed his mild thunder on the age-old hush, ceased as suddenly as it had begun. From the top-most branch of a cedar rampike a kingfisher hurled itself like a plummet to shatter the glassy surface of the water, then emerged, having missed its intended prey, and once more took up its vigil on top of the dead cedar.

David could see a maze of deep trails, that, throughout the centuries, heavy animals: moose, deer, and caribou, had worn in the soft tundra. The whole scene bespoke antiquity, a build-up that had taken thousands of years since the last ice sheath had made its slow retreat.

Each scene was familiar, a part of that unforgettable past when, first as a captive, and then as honoured guest, he had sojourned among the Maliseets of the Saint John River.

Fourteen years! What power those two words had to conjure up the past; of which two days, a mere forty-eight hours, and of that perhaps six hours, that were to stand out in his life like a flame.

They brought back the vision of the girl seated beside her father in the little Maliseet chapel, the pure oval of her face, her hair, her eyes.

He even remembered the abbreviated Latin inscription on the slate stone hung on the wall in the interior of the chapel, which in full read: "*Deo Optimo Maximo. In honorem Divi Joannis Baptistae Hoc Templum Posuerunt Anno Domini MDCC XVII. Malecitae Missionis Procurator Joanne Loyard, Societatis, Jesu Sacerdote.*" And in the left hand corner, "*P. Darelou.*" (To God, Most Excellent Most High, in honor of Saint John Baptist, the Maliseets erected this Church, A.D. 1717, while Jean Loyard, a priest of the Society of Jesus, was superintendent of the Mission.)

And the day following, when he had caught Jeanne Chartier the trout; again, his visit to the priest's house that night, when to Father Germain, Monsieur Chartier, and Jeanne he had told of his abduction and years of slavery. Finally, the feeling of heartsickness and loneliness that had swept over him like a dull pain, as the canoe carrying her and Monsieur Chartier became mere specks on the river.

Well, he had returned hoping to find her, and, if she were free, and would accept him, to bestow upon her all the affection that had burned in him so faithfully these many years.

He had found her surrounded by her few fellow refugees, all living in the constant fear that any day might see some English officer come to command them to report to the fort at the river's mouth, and from thence be sent into exile, as had others of their compatriots.

Their anxiety, as well as their poverty, appalled him. Their suspicion that he had come to spy on them under the cloak of a renewal of an old acquaintance with their leader had vanished.

He felt that even Etienne d'Amours, though still frankly hostile, now realized that his coming had been innocent of any intended harm. As for the others, they were now friendly and grateful for his care of them during the sickness.

And Jeanne—she had told him she would never cease to pray for him. Otherwise she was as far removed from him as ever. He had intended leaving Medaweska the day following the priest's arrival. But the need for fuel and meat, both of which were a serious lack, as well as his reluctance to tear himself away from the woman he loved—even though he felt convinced she could not return his affection—had impelled him to stay longer.

He heaved a deep sigh. Well, he had helped cut wood fuel to last until those now convalescing were strong enough to work. If this hunt proved successful, there would be no further excuse he could give them for remaining. It was tragic, and inevitable. He would return to Aberdeen. His friend and partner would mourn with him: and that would be as it ought; for their affection was deep and abiding.

33

Suddenly, from afar, there drifted to the Scot's ears the call of the cow moose. The blood raced through his veins. Was it actually one of the animals, or had it been Tomah who had sent out those forlorn and impelling notes? Again it came. It floated over the great barren, over the dead water, the very essence of age-old primitive longing, to die away finally in a mere thread of sound.

For a brief space of time a profound silence filled the wilderness. Then, from the enclosing palisade of evergreens that bordered the brook up which d'Amours and the Micmac had gone, there came the deep, raucous bark of a bull moose.

David glanced hurriedly at the pan of his gun, saw that it was full of powder, pulled back the lock with its enclosed flint, and swung the piece around until it pointed across the dead water.

Again the air was split with that hair-raising bark; yet not so close this time. He heard a dead tree crash, then silence.

He waited. Suddenly, from up the brook there came the discharge of a gun—D'Amours' or the Micmac's, he felt sure. He would like to have had a shot at the beast; but actually it mattered not who killed it. Meat, fresh meat, was the urgent need of the settlers at Medaweska.

There came a crash directly opposite among the tamaracks and spruces, then a huge bull swung into view. It raced to the bank of the dead water, sprang in, spurning up the water as it swam, its enormous antlers reaching far back over its shoulders and on either side.

The Scot hesitated. Would he fire at this moving target, or wait until it had reached the hard bottom of the crossing place, and got to its feet? He waited. A few seconds later it found footing only about fifty yards distant.

David's gun barrel wobbled crazily, finally steadied. Aiming directly behind the beast's shoulder, he pressed the trigger. There was a thunderous discharge; the moose sprang upward, and falling backward threw the water a dozen feet high. It gave a deep groan, quivered a few moments, and floated lifeless in the now muddy water.

David was reaching feverishly for his powder horn, when his eye caught an object emerging from the mouth of the brook. Then he saw it was d'Amours in his canoe. He was alone. He was crouched on his knees in the stern, with each sweep of his paddle lifting the bow high out of the water. He swung to his right, came in a diagonal course towards David. Suddenly, the craft struck a partly submerged tree that had fallen into the water at some far time, and in the twinkling of an eye it turned completely over, throwing d'Amours into the water. He sank, came up, his hands beating the water into foam in his efforts to reach the canoe. He did manage to get near enough to catch hold of the stern, but it slipped from his grasp and shot farther away. Again his hands frantically beat the water.

Meanwhile, realizing the Acadian did not know how to swim, David was running along the bank. He had thrown off his coat, waistcoat, and hat. Coming opposite d'Amours he tore off his shoes, and, crying to the struggling Acadian that he was coming, he slid down the bank into the shallow shore water. Luckily it chanced to be the crossing place Tomah had told him about, else he would have sunk in water and mud to his middle. But the bottom was firm. He waded out several yards, then began swimming with strong, quick strokes towards the struggling d'Amours.

The Acadian had again reached the canoe: again it slipped from his clutching fingers. His eyes were wild, his face distorted with fear as he endeavoured to keep himself from going under.

David was close to him now. "Keep cool, Etienne!" he shouted. If the Acadian heard he was too terror-stricken to heed. He was sinking a second time as David reached out, grasped him by the shoulder, and began treading water. Now ensued a struggle between them: d'Amours trying to fling both arms about David's neck, David evading them, and shouting to d'Amours to put his hands on his shoulders, and he would get him to shore. He might as well have shouted at the sun.

Finally, with a quick twist, he broke away from d'Amours, and mustering all his strength, dealt him a blow between the eyes that stunned him. He flung up his arms with a low gasp, was sinking when David seized him by the shoulder, and holding his face above water, struggled with him towards the shore.

It was only a few rods. But the Acadian was heavy, and the Scot almost exhausted when finally he got footing. He tugged with all his remaining strength, drew d'Amours behind him towards the depression where the brook had worn its bed. He prayed that the fellow would remain quiet until he was able to reach the bank, now only a few feet distant. He gave another tug and reached it. The water was less than a foot deep. He paused a few moments to regain his breath, now coming in hoarse gasps; then, reaching down he put both arms about d'Amours, by a supreme effort lifted him up bodily, and thrust him forward until he was resting on the sandy bed of the brook.

Now he put up one knee, then the other, and, catching hold of a tamarack limb above him, pulled himself to his feet. He took a few steps forward and, grasping d'Amours by the shoulders, dragged him farther inland. Kneeling down he felt d'Amours' pulse. It was quite strong; even as David started to rise, d'Amours opened his eyes and gazed wildly up at him.

34

It had been an exhausting affair for David; and, now that d'Amours had regained consciousness, he muttered a fervent thank God and incontinently sat down opposite him. He felt weak and cold. His teeth began to hit one against the other, and shivers ran up and down his spine.

Slowly d'Amours raised himself to a sitting posture. He had lost his cap, and his wet, mud-clotted hair straggled over his brow. His left eye was swollen; from his right nostril a little trail of blood trickled into his black beard. He was a pitiful and grotesque figure, his breath coming quickly from between lips parted over even white teeth. He stared dully at David.

"You are feeling better now, Etienne?"

The Acadian nodded slowly, raised a hand and wiped the blood from his chin.

Thus they sat a few moments looking at each other. Cold shivers swept David from head to foot as with an ague. He got to his feet, found his jacket and waistcoat, and put them on; finally his shoes, and forced his wet, stockinged feet into them. Coming back he saw that d'Amours had got up, gone to a dead tamarack, and was breaking the limbs within his reach. David went to another tamarack and followed his example.

When each had an armful they carried them back to the dry bed of the brook—the only place suitable for a fire—and threw them down. Then they went for more. The exercise partly warmed David. D'Amours worked with feverish haste. Save for his bruised face, he now seemed none the worse for all he had undergone. He spoke no words. They found a fallen cedar; between them dragged it to the place they had put the other wood.

Now d'Amours took his knife from its sheath and whittled a little pile of shavings; which done, he placed sticks over them. He looked up at David, "Your powder-horn, Monsieur, and your gun?" he said.

David went to where he had left them when he had fired at the moose, picked them up and returned to D'Amours.

"Is it loaded, Monsieur?"

"No, Etienne."

"I heard Monsieur fire," said d'Amours. "I shot at the moose; it ran. I decided it would cross the dead water towards this place." He ceased, took the powder horn, poured a little of the powder on his shavings. Then he filled the pan of the gun, pulled back the lock, and holding the pan of the piece sideways, close to the shavings, he pulled the trigger. There was a flash of flame as the flint struck the steel, followed by a second flash and black smoke as the powder on the shavings ignited. In a few moments the dry wood was burning freely.

"That was a clever idea! I would not have thought to do it," said David admiringly.

D'Amours made no comment. He heaped more dry branches on his fire, seized hold of the cedar log, swung it into position on one side of the blaze to serve as a backlog. As David began shivering again, d'Amours turned to him and said:

"Do you sit here and get warm, Monsieur. I will bring more wood— No, Monsieur," as David began to protest that he would help, "Please to get warm. I can do it alone." He was about to turn away when David said:

"Where did you leave the Micmac, Etienne?"

"He is up the brook, beyond where I was. He will wait; the others will pick him up," he said briefly. And without further words went about his work.

David sat down as close as he could get to the blaze without burning himself. He took off his shoes, set them to dry, removed his stockings, wrung the water from them, hung them on two sticks he forced into the sand in front of the fire, and now sat with his bare feet close to the comforting heat. But, although they were soon warm, the rest of his body was so cold he began shivering anew.

From time to time, Etienne returned with more dry tamarack and cedar. Finally, after half an hour's work he said, "We have enough for the present." And stood with his back to the fire.

"You had better dry your foot things too," said David.

The Acadian made no reply. Finally, he turned, facing David, and said in a husky voice, "You saved my life, Monsieur."

"Luckily I am able to swim," said David lightly. Then added, "I'm so sorry I had to strike you, Etienne; but it was the only thing to do."

"The blow was nothing: it does not now hurt. As for my life," continued d'Amours, "it is not worth saving."

"Oh, I say, why not?" protested David. "If the situation had been reversed, you would have done the same for me."

An anguished look overspread d'Amours' face. "No, Monsieur, I would have let you drown. I would have been happy to know you were at the bottom of the dead water."

"Oh," said David, greatly shocked, "that is too bad! Of course I do not understand—"

"Yes," broke in the Acadian vehemently, "it is bad—bad! There is even more, Monsieur. But let me tell you: That day by the waterfall, when we fought, I told you I would kill you—and I meant it. It was my wish. I choked you with my hands while you were insensible. Then your Indian came. It was the good God who sent him." The Acadian paused, crossed himself, then repeated, "Yes, it was the good God who sent him.

"It was this way, Monsieur: It was not only that I hated you for belonging to the race that had wronged my people, but, too, it was because of Jeanne Chartier. I had loved her for long. But she cared nothing for Etienne d'Amours…only…only as a friend, as a brother Acadian. And then, you came. I stood behind a tree and watched you both, heard what you both said, and I was mad with jealousy that she could love you, and not me—"

"Oh," interjected David, "but you are mistaken, Etienne. She does not love *me*. Quite the contrary: she told me to leave Medaweska."

"Love," said Etienne d'Amours, "speaks a strange language. You were—are—blind, that is all."

"No," protested David. "I wish it were otherwise, but you are wholly wrong. She loves, but it is not I."

"Ah," said Etienne, "I have heard that the English are stupid. Pardon me, you are a Scot, but Monsieur is no exception. And worse, he is both stupid and blind." He ceased, turned to the fire, put on another log. Turning again to David, he continued:

"Monsieur Cameron, one day you asked me to take your hand. I refused. Will you take it now?"

"Gladly," cried David. He sprang to his feet, and grasping the hand of the outstretched Acadian, wrung it heartily.

"Thank you, Monsieur. I…" The voice of d'Amours shook with emotion. He continued huskily, "I am now at peace with myself, and with you. It is good."

David turned, looked out on the water and said, "You have lost your gun, Etienne; your canoe is out there bottom-up; but," and he pointed to the moose floating in the muddy shore water, "we have fresh meat, and far more precious, we have found friendship."

"Yes, Monsieur."

"Hark," said David, "There go two shots.. another! Let us hope that the others have had good luck. And now, Etienne," he added, "do you empty your moccasins of water, and wring out your socks."

"Not so, Monsieur," said Etienne. "On the trail I have been wet many times. I have broken through weak ice in deep water and have been almost frozen. But Etienne d'Amours does not take the cold." He paused, added, "It will be well for us if I now get more wood. The others will be late coming, and we shall have to stay here the night. See, the sun is already getting low."

"I will help," said David. "Yes, Etienne," as d'Amours protested that there was no need. So he forced his feet into his still damp shoes, leaving his stockings to dry further, and followed the Acadian.

Together they found fallen tamaracks and cedar, which they bore to the fire. They found a big cedar stump, the centre rotted, but the outer shell sound and dry as tinder. With great labour they tore this off and ranked it beside the other fuel. Finally d'Amours said, "It is enough, Monsieur," and sat down in front of the fire.

The sun sank nearer the horizon, and with its waning the air was more chilly. They crouched side by side in the dry bed of the brook; their garments steamed. But in spite of the heat, David still felt cold, and he turned his back, now his front to the blaze. Finally,

realizing that he was hungry, he got his knapsack, and taking out
the small cakes of corn bread he had brought with him, he gave
one to d'Amours.

35

The sun reached a group of tall pines on the distant ridge, their scraggy limbs silhouetted in sharp relief against the horizon. For a few moments it appeared to stand upon the tops of the pines, then, like the scene on a drop in a theatre, it slowly slid downwards, seeming to swell and undulate like molten metal in an enormous cauldron. Then it disappeared from view.

High in the west a few fleecy clouds, caught in the afterglow, sailed in unison across the sky, like a fleet of rose-pink ships bound to some distant haven far to the eastward.

David watched them entranced until their colour faded, and night, like a drawn curtain, settled over the wilderness; then, more to himself than to his companion, he said. "Ah, the mystery of it; the untranslatable mystery of it!" He remained silent a few moments, then again spoke:

"It has always been thus, century after century, long before the Indians, coming from the far west, discovered this land of Acadia, and, finding that it was good, pushed their frail canoes up rivers, dead waters and lakes, and gave them names in their beautiful and descriptive tongue." He ceased, and d'Amours said:

"And then came our French, and they too found that it was good."

"Yes," agreed David.

D'Amours was staring with brooding eyes into the fire. When next he spoke, gone was the hostility of previous occasions. His voice was low, charged with a hopeless sadness that profoundly stirred the young Scot:

"Then the English came to Acadia; and because our mother country failed us, and they were many, and well armed, they finally subdued us. Their portion of America was big enough, but they must have more! It is too bad, Monsieur."

David remained silent a few moments. He could have told d'Amours that the English based a prior claim to America on the voyages of the Cabots. But it would have involved going into the history of the last two hundred and fifty years; the rivalries between monarchs anxious for territorial acquisitions; of merchant adventurers seeking outlets for trade; the employment of the different Indian tribes in warfare by both sides, with subsequent retaliation for barbarities committed; the hates engendered in consequence thereof.

It would have done no good to argue the case. He knew that while Etienne grieved over the loss of New France, it was that of the country north of the Bay of Fundy (as included in the ancient boundaries of Acadia), and the almost wholesale banishment of the inhabitants south of the Bay, that he especially resented; that the massacre of the people of St. Ann's, and the deporting of the Acadians who had come to the Saint John from Quebec, had fired his indignation. The rest had been war, and he was too intelligent not to realize that harsh measures only too often accompany it. But whatever there had been of injustice, or by whomever consummated, David felt sure that time, in her own way, would compensate the oppressed by at least evaluating in their true light the motives that caused their perpetrators to impose them. He now turned to d'Amours, and said gently:

"The Chinese have a saying that time adjusts all things. May it not be, my friend, that eventually, when passions shall have cooled, your people will return, and the two races abide together in harmony, as the good God intended they should?"

The Acadian devoutly crossed himself. Then, with a hand cupped to his ear, "I hear the paddles, Monsieur; Tomah and the others are coming."

Quickly he got to his feet, followed by David. They went to the edge of the bank, stood there waiting. In a few moments they saw the canoes, dark shapes upon the blacker surface of the water. They paused opposite the brook up which Etienne and the Micmac had gone. One of the canoes turned in to the shore, and the watchers saw the dim figure of the Micmac enter it. Then it came on. Coming to d'Amours' upturned craft both canoes paused, and the two watchers heard voices raised in excited questionings.

David called out: "It is all right. Etienne is here!"

He heard one of the Acadians give a low exclamation. They paddled towards the shore, saw the moose in the water, paused again, talked a little, then came on.

Reaching the bank they clambered up it, secured the canoes, and clustered about David and d'Amours, asking questions.

It was d'Amours who briefly described the accident. "I had shot at the moose. I do not know if I hit it. It ran. I knew it would try to cross the dead water at the crossing. I jumped in my canoe, paddled down the brook, and was coming to this side when the canoe struck something and upset. You know I do not swim. I would have drowned but for Monsieur Cameron who came and brought me to shore. To him I owe my life. I have given thanks to God—and to him." And he reverently crossed himself.

The other hunters had killed two moose; a cow and a bull. They had only time to bleed them and remove the entrails when dark set in. They brought back the liver of one, and would go back in the morning, skin and quarter the meat. In the meanwhile, by the light of the campfire, the moose d'Amours had wounded—for such proved to be the case—and David had finally killed, was towed to shore and quickly dressed.

A little later, having taken the two canoes from the water, they placed them on one side of the fire to form a windbreak. Now they sliced some of the liver, roasting it on wooden spits held over coals raked to the forefront. They ate sparingly, well knowing it was not wise to use much before it was thoroughly chilled.

<h1 style="text-align:center">36</h1>

To David the night seemed endless. For a long while he lay listening to the talk of his companions as they described in detail their experiences of the afternoon. Finally he dropped off to sleep. How long, he knew not, but he awoke shaking with cold, his teeth chattering. The fire was burning brightly. He could see Tomah, pipe in mouth, seated beside it, immobile as a statue. Then, as he spoke the Chief's name, Tomah turned and said in Maliseet:

"*Ta-ka-o* (cold), P'sazum?"

"*Ah-ha*," faltered David.

The Indian got quickly to his feet. Picking up his own blanket he held it before the fire.

Realizing what he was about to do, David spoke! "*Kadama* (no), my father."

The Chief made no reply and David, knowing that any further protests would be futile, held his peace.

Soon the blanket was almost smoking hot. Tomah came over, wrapped it about the Scot's shoulders and hips, binding it with a piece of rawhide.

Said David, "*Wul-e-wun* (thank you), my father. It feels good."

Thereafter, throughout the long night, the Chief ministered to him—now his own warmed jacket, now his blanket reheated and placed about him.

David slept but fitfully. He had frightening dreams; now in fancy battling with Etienne d'Amours in the dead water; again trying to free his arms to ward off a big lynx that persisted in clawing at his throat.

When morning finally dawned, and he was thoroughly awake, he realized that he was very ill. Chills ran up and down his back, even while he seemed burning. He noted that Tomah was crouched before the fire stirring something in one of the pewter mugs.

David got slowly to his feet, found his head whirling. He would have fallen had it not been that d'Amours sprang up and supported him. "Monsieur is sick," he said gently.

"I am afraid so, Etienne. I will lie down again, please."

Now Tomah rose and, the mug in his hand, came and knelt beside him. "Drink, P'sazum," he said, holding it to David's lips.

Slowly the Scot sipped the hot, aromatic drink. He knew that it was made from the leaves of the Labrador shrub; an old, old remedy used by the Indians from time immemorial. When the last of the stuff had trickled from the cup, Tomah said in Maliseet, "*Ek-pa-hawk.*" (Which is to say, it is done dropping.) Then he added, "It is good medicine, my son."

"*Wul-e-wun, N'me-tukws* (thank you, my father)," murmured David.

He knew little of what followed. The drink, slightly narcotic, soon induced a more peaceful sleep.

37

Some time later, he knew not how long, he was picked up by strong arms, and opening his eyes, saw that it was d'Amours and Antoine Cormier who had lifted him.

They carried him to the bank, put him into the waiting arms of Tomah and the Micmac, standing in the water below, who gently placed him flat in the bottom of the canoe, blankets beneath and over him.

It was all inexpressibly silly to have succumbed like this, after a mere few minutes in the water. Then he thought it could not be wholly that; in all probability he had caught the sickness from Monsieur Chartier and the others. But it did not matter. He was now going back to Medaweska, and to Jeanne…

He closed his eyes, felt the canoe move forward, heard the rhythmic dip of Tomah's paddle, and again drifted off to sleep.

During one of his moments of consciousness he asked Tomah if the others were coming.

"Bye and bye," answered the Chief. "Now they go to skin and cut up the moose. We take two quarters with us, P'sazum."

They came to the brook up which they had poled yesterday—was it only yesterday? It seemed to David much longer than that: a week, at least. The water quickened. He could feel the canoe swerve as Tomah guided it around some fallen log, or took a sudden bend of the stream.

Again he slept, and dreamed all manner of strange things. Finally, he was on board his own ship the *Sheila Grahme*, and she was bucking heavy seas in the English Channel.

At the moment, Tomah was standing in the stern of the heavily-laden canoe, his shoulders slightly stooped as, having discarded his paddle for the long spruce-wood setting pole, he worked his way through the boulder-strewn rapids of the lower Medaweska.

His dark eyes saw each bulging swell that denoted rocks beneath, or those projecting above the surface. With one end of his pole against the bottom of the stream he would snub the wild charge of the canoe, hold it to a quivering standstill, then ease it around the seen or hidden boulders in the narrow and tortuous channel. Then he would allow it to spring forward again, like an eager race horse that has been momentarily checked. The curling back-wash rushed almost level with the gunwales. His heart leaped in tune with and joyed in the wild cacophony of the rapids. Yet he worked with care, with the cool confidence born of forty years of conflict with many a turbulent and dangerous river.

He could now see the Saint John, or, as the Maliseet call it, the *Wul-ahs-tukw*, and the log cabins of the Acadians clustered on the left hand bank of the Medaweska.

A few more rods and he was in quieter water. He swung the bow of the canoe shorewards, facing up stream, brought it close to the beach, stepped out, grasped the gunwale, and drew it in until the bottom touched the loose gravel.

"P'sazum," he said, touching David's arm.

The Scot opened his eyes, gazed up at the dark face, and recognizing him, asked dully:

"Where are we, my father?"

"Medaweska," was Tomah's brief reply. Then he added, "We are at the *Odanic*, P'sazum." By which he meant they had arrived at the Acadian settlement.

"Ah!" breathed David, "that is good." With difficulty he raised himself to a sitting posture.

The Chief took his hand, carefully helped him out to the beach, where David stood swaying weakly until Tomah had drawn up the canoe. This done, and with Tomah's supporting arm about him, they slowly walked up the beach beyond which stood the log cabins of the Acadians. They were seen by the priest and Noël Thibedeau, who both hastened forward. To the priest's anxious enquiry, Tomah said, 'P'sazum is sick. *Mutjeg'n* (very bad)."

They took him to the cabin of Raoul Chartier. Jeanne rose from a stool, came quickly to them, sudden fear in her eyes. "What has happened?" she asked anxiously, thinking that Etienne had done him injury.

It was the priest who spoke: "It is the sickness, my daughter. We have brought him here, for your care."

A wan smile curved David's lips. "If Mademoiselle will be so kind," he faltered.

She ran to her bunk, pulled down the blankets, arranged the moss-filled pillow, then swept back to them. "He shall stay in my bed," she said to Tomah and the priest. Then to David, "Come, Monsieur."

38

The priest gave him quinine and senna tea.

On the second day David bled at the nose and developed a bad cough.

"It is the sickness that killed so many of our people a long time ago," said Tomah. And he went to the dead water beyond the waterfall for lily roots.

When he returned he macerated one of them with the pole of his axe and made a poultice. This he heated on the flat stone in the fireplace. When it was ready, it was Jeanne who opened David's shirt, rubbed fish oil on his chest, then applied the poultice.

Tomah made a second poultice, so that as soon as one had cooled they had a hot one ready to apply. Again he went out, to return a few minutes later with small branches of the white pine. He put some of them with water in the skillet. As it simmered he gently stirred the mass with a wooden spoon.

"It is good medicine," he said to Jeanne. "My grandmother she told me about it a long time ago, when I was a *skin-o-sis* (small boy). Might be it will make my son well."

When the pine branches had steeped to Tomah's satisfaction, he strained the liquid, then asked Jeanne if she had any maple syrup.

She nodded, ran and got it for him. He poured some of the syrup into the medicine he had made, stirred it thoroughly. After it had cooled, he raised the Scot's head, put the cup to his lips, and said, "Drink, my son."

Without opening his eyes, David slowly sipped it. Then Tomah lowered his head to the pillow.

Monsieur Chartier was now rapidly improving, but still weak. He had been going out for a short walk each day. But for the most part of his time he sat in his chair, or reposed on his bunk. A dozen times each day he enquired of Jeanne or the priest if David had yet sweat. He had previously told Father Germain of David's plans for establishing truck houses on the river. When he finished the priest said:

"That is good, my son. It is what we need. And if his influence with the authorities is great enough—as you suggest is possible—it may mean future happiness for us all."

Several times Etienne silently entered the cabin, and crossing the floor to where David lay on the bunk, stood looking down at him, his lips moving in silent prayer. Then, crossing himself, he would go out again. Once he said to the priest, "Will he get better, Father?" And the priest replied, "He is in God's hands, Etienne. I have said a mass for him, and also instructed all the people here to pray."

Most of the time David lay with closed eyes; when he did occasionally open them, it was without recognizing those who were nearby. Any muttered words were unintelligible. They came from lips parched and dry. Often spasms of coughing shook his whole body.

39

Five days passed. Darkness had again fallen over Medaweska. Jeanne set the table for the evening meal. Moose meat had been boiled in one of the iron skillets.

Etienne came in, sat beside Monsieur Chartier on an up-drawn bench, Tomah and Jeanne opposite. There was little conversation, and that only in subdued voices. If the sick man stirred, or muttered in his delirium, Jeanne was on her feet and rushed to his side to feel his brow. Then she returned to her place as silently as she had gone.

When the meal was ended Etienne gathered up the few dishes. Having washed and dried them, he seated himself beside the fireplace and lighted his pipe, often pausing to steal glances towards the sick man, or to return his gaze to watch what Tomah was doing.

The Chief had gone out during the afternoon and brought in a bundle of cat-tails from a nearby swamp, some blue pottery clay, and a little coarse sand. He now quickly fashioned a round ball of this clay and sand, and with the mass in his left palm, he pressed his right fist against the top, hollowing it with quick, rotating movements. Glancing up at Etienne's intent eyes, he said, "Tomah is making an Indian lamp in the old-time way." He bent again to his task. Often he paused to restore the outer uneven surface with a little wooden paddle he had made earlier. Then the hollowing-out process was resumed. Finally, when this was done to his liking, he placed the bowl bottom-end on the bench beside him and rotated it gently until it was perfectly flat. It was about five inches in diameter across the top, and three inches deep. Now, with a low grunt of satisfaction, he raked back the coals from the front of the fireplace and carefully set the bowl on the hot stones. Thereafter, he occasionally turned it so that the clay would dry out evenly on all sides. He said to Etienne:

"My people make bowls long before the white man bring us kettles, and iron pots. Made them little, made them big. Use them for cooking. Use little one like this for lamp. Call it *B's-ukw-han-mogan-sis*. Need them for light, when squaw have young at night time. Some time we put in fish oil; some time fat from animals. Put in cattail some time for wick; some time alder stick. Alder inside it like punk. It sucks up the oil. Yes," he added, "it makes a good light."

Etienne nodded to show he understood. Jeanne came forward. "I need a warm poultice, Tomah," she said.

As she went back to the sick bunk the door opened to admit the priest. He crossed at once to David's side, took his wrist and felt the pulse. Then he said to Jeanne,

"It is time for more quinine, my daughter."

When the powder was dissolved, he spoke to David, "It is time for the medicine, Monsieur Cameron."

At his name David opened his eyes. "Yes," he whispered. They lifted his head; he swallowed the quinine, and they eased him back to the pillow.

The priest spoke to Raoul Chartier. Then he went to the door. Jeanne followed him. "Is he worse, Father?"

"No, my daughter; nor is he better than a few hours ago. He has not sweat. When he does, we shall know that the fever has turned. But courage, my daughter." And added, "You should have rest. You must have sleep. I shall return later and take your place."

"It is not necessary, Father. *I* will watch. Do not fear for me. I am strong. If anything should happen to him—if he should die… Goodnight, Father."

He gave her a quick look. Her unfinished sentence disquieted him. He merely said, "I shall return later, and give him more quinine."

Etienne soon followed. But before going he told Jeanne she had but to call if she needed him; he would sleep on Tomah's bed under the canoe.

The girl went over and sat down beside David. By the dim light cast by the fire she could see his flushed face, and hear his quick breathing. When he coughed she involuntarily clasped her hands to her own throat, as though, by her act, she could ease his spasms.

She touched his hot brow. Would the sweat never begin? Her hand sought her beads and crucifix. "Good Saint Ann, pray for him," she whispered, as she quickly moved the beads along the little chain.

Tomah was sitting in front of the fire. He had covered his little bowl with hot ashes and live cinders, which he now renewed from time to time. The flames lighted up his hawk-like features. Between his teeth was his little pipe, the smoke curling in rings above his head, that was shaved save for a short scalp lock, twisted and tied with a bit of rawhide.

The girl felt the poultice; rose and went to Tomah. "Heat the other one, *Ne-dup* (friend)," she said.

Obediently he lifted the second poultice from the hearth and placed it carefully on the flat stone that had served their need so many times.

When it was sufficiently hot he took it to her. She removed the poultice on David's chest and replaced it with the hot one. She looked up at the Chief, standing silently beside her, and her voice was tremulous as she said, "Is there nothing more we can do, Tomah?"

He remained silent a few moments. Finally, he nodded and said, "Tomah will try. Tomah is *Me-ta-o-lin*. He will try to drive away the evil spirit that has caused the sickness," and, crossing the floor, picked up the remainder of the clay from which he had fashioned his lamp.

She half turned to watch him; saw his long brown fingers kneading it, pressing this way and that. He worked for several minutes. At last he came to her and held out the thing he had fashioned that she might see it.

What she saw horrified her. It was a crude likeness of a monstrous creature that resembled a human face. The ears stuck out like bats' wings; the eyes were ugly hollows in the puffed-out cheeks, and from the thick lips protruded what was meant for a tongue, but forked like that of a snake's.

"What is it, Tomah?" she whispered.

"It is the bad spirit that makes the sickness," he answered.

He walked to the fireplace, turned, facing her, the image that makes sickness held in his left palm on a level with, and at arm's length from his shoulder. Then he began speaking in his own tongue. His voice was at first modulated to a low sing-song. He besought the great Sagûm Glooskap to see what he was doing, and help him subdue the spirit that makes sickness, causing the death of strong and good people. Now his voice rose. He poured out abuse and invective at the image. It was a thief that stole little children, male and female; and mature mankind, male and female. It destroyed babes in their mothers' wombs. It robbed the tribe of strong warriors, so that those remaining became the easy prey of their enemies.

He used no swear words as known to Europeans; for the Indians have none in their language. But he consigned the spirit that causes sickness to the fury of fire, and the depths of swift waters. He gave it to the thunderbolt that rends great rocks and trees; to the freezing breath of winter.

His voice rose higher until it filled the room, and his normally noble and placid countenance was transformed and etched with deep furrows, while his dark eyes glittered like those of one under the spell of religious fervour.

The girl stirred uneasily. She had heard of the Shamanistic rites practised by Indian witch doctors, and of others who were *me-ta-o-lin* (magic workers), and she was afraid of she knew not what. She tried to withdraw her eyes from him, but the impelling wizardry of his voice would not allow her. It was as though she were under the spell of some strange and daemonic force that was robbing her of poise, even of sanity itself. Her fingers groped for and found her beads.

Barely was she conscious that her father had awakened, was sitting on the side of his bunk, watching Tomah; but he spoke no words. The door opened and Etienne d'Amours entered. Closing it behind him, he stood gazing awesomely at the Chief's distorted face, and listening to his wild chant.

The priest came in, hastily crossed the floor to the girl's side, bent and looked at David's face, felt his brow. Then he straightened and let his eyes rest on the Chief.

The girl was glad he had come.

Father Germain was shocked. Had then, all the years of Christian teaching of his predecessors, and of his own ministry among the aborigines, availed so little, that they could so readily revert to their heathen practices? But he too spoke not. For he well knew any words he might say would be futile; and furthermore, the proud Chief would consider them an insult, not only to his dignity, but also to one who had inherited from countless forefathers the power of *me-ta-o-lin* that is the envy and superstitious awe of those not so endowed.

Now, holding the spirit that causes sickness high above his head, the Chief began dancing, his body swaying from side to side, his moccasined feet making only a shuffling sound on the planked floor. As he swayed this way and that his words took on a keening wail that echoed from the log rafters which supported the low roof.

Finally the song grew slower, ended. He lowered his arm and placed the image on the bench beside him. He picked up his pipe, solemnly filled it, and bending to the fire scooped up a live coal, put the stem in his mouth, and pulled on it until the tobacco was alight.

Now he again lifted the image of the spirit that causes sickness, and, filling his mouth with smoke, he blew it against the face of the thing. Three times he repeated this performance; then he restored the pipe to the mantel, and again setting the image on the bench, he crouched beside it, and recited three times the word: "*mut-jeg-o!*" At the final "*mut-jeg-o!*" he clenched his right fist and brought it down with a thud on the image, flattening it. Then, rising quickly with the mass of clay in his hand, he strode to the door, opened it and flung it outside. Hastily slamming the door, he came back. Drawing his tall figure to its full height he said simply, looking at Jeanne:

"My son will now get well."

For some strange reason she believed him. But she interpreted his next act as an admission that, however sanguine his faith in his *me-ta-o-lin*, he was not above supplementing it by accepted therapeutic measures: for he picked up the mug that contained some of the white-pine tea he had made, and brought it to her.

She laid her hand on David's brow, spoke his name.

He opened his eyes, touched his tongue to his dry lips, and whispered, "What is it, Jeanne?"

"You are now to take the medicine, P'sazum."

The priest raised his shoulders. Slowly David drank; muttered a low thank you.

They gently lowered him again to the pillow. Father Germain went to the table and dissolved some of the quinine. He looked at his watch by the light from the fireplace, and said to the girl, "We will give it to him in an hour, my daughter." Then added, "Do you lie down and rest. I will stay and watch."

But she would not have it so. "No, no," she protested. "It is my—a woman's birthright to tend the sick."

She said it with such a tone of finality that he did not urge her more. "In an hour, then, my daughter. And renew the poultice often."

He touched her head, murmuring a blessing. He was troubled in spirit. If the Scot got better, what would be the outcome of the girl's all too apparent affection for him, and of his for her? Else he would not have journeyed all this distance from Medowktek.

He knew that on the occasion of her stay at the Augustine convent her relative, the Mother Abbess, had endeavoured to exact from her a promise eventually to join the sisterhood, that band of noble women, who, renouncing the ways of the world, devote their lives to things spiritual, teaching and caring for the ills of suffering humanity.

He too had spoken to the girl. But her attitude at the time had been that so long as her father lived, she could not leave him. That, he was now convinced, would be her answer to this foreigner for whom he also had an affection. And, too, they were of different faith, did there exist no other barriers.

Being human, and young, they would suffer for a time. But later, when her father had passed from this troubled world, she, submitting to the divine will, would find peace. He sighed, made the sign of the cross, and left the cabin.

Tomah had placed his earthen lamp on the table and poured into it some of the fish oil. Now, cutting one of the cat-tails into four-inch portions, he dipped one of them into the oil, stood it upright in the bowl, and lighted it. It burned brightly, like a candle, shedding a soft, friendly glow.

"It is beautiful, Tomah," whispered Jeanne.

"*Ah-ha*," he agreed, "*Wul-e-na-gwit, B's-ukw-han-mogan.*" (Yes, it is a good lamp.) Then he heated a new poultice.

A little later he spread his blanket on the floor in front of the fireplace, and, with a block of wood for a pillow, laid himself down.

But he did not sleep. The girl knew it. The room was charged with his awakeness, and she was glad. She felt not so alone with him awake and with the cheerful improvised candle aglow.

Nor would *she* sleep, though her eyes smarted and she was weary in soul and body. With her eyes on the little crucifix above the bunk she began telling her beads again, repeating over and over: "Good Saint Ann, pray for him," the beads slipping one by one from her fingers. When she finished the last one she began again; this time her lips framing a whispered prayer to the virgin mother of Christ: "Mary, mother, pray for him."

Suddenly, she paused, and reaching out laid her hand on David's brow. Then, with a muted exclamation of delight, she sprang to her feet and swept across the floor to Tomah.

He was on his feet with one cat-like movement.

She grasped him by both arms. "Tomah, Tomah," she cried, "it is the sweat at last!" Then the glad tears rained down her cheeks.

The Chief said with calm assurance, "It was the *me-ta-o-lin.*" Reaching David's side he touched his brow. "*Ah-ha*, he will get well. *Ka-loo-ut* (good)," and without further words went back, filled and lighted his pipe. Putting more wood on the fire, he sat down on his blanket, his dark eyes fixed complacently on the leaping flames. His son would live. It was good.

The girl reached out and felt David's wrist. Yes, the pulse was no longer hurried: his breath was coming more evenly. She bent her head and gently touched her lips to his cheek, then straightened as he opened his eyes and looked up at her. She felt her face flaming to the roots of her hair.

A little smile curved his lips. He remained silent a few moments, finally said, "I had a beautiful dream, Jeanne. I think I shall now get better. I will go to sleep again, and…it may be that I shall dream it all over again."

"Yes, P'sazum," she murmured; "but first you must take more of the good medicine Tomah has brewed for you."

40

It was a week later. David Cameron was so much improved he was now able to be up two or three hours each afternoon. At present he was sitting in front of the fireplace. Raoul Chartier had gone to Pierre Robechaud's cabin to talk. Tomah and Etienne d'Amours were in the woods hunting; for though the three moose they had killed earlier were sufficient for the needs of the settlement for another two months, the long winter ahead would necessitate a still greater supply.

Jeanne Chartier was busy sweeping the cabin floor with a broom made by lashing to a handle a bundle of alder branches. She worked quietly, going into every corner and under the bunks, as a good housekeeper should. As she worked she sang in a low voice the deathless love of *A la Claire Fontaine*.

> Unto a fountain clear
> I went one summer day,
> So cool I found the water
> I plunged into the spray,
> > A long time have I loved you,
> > And I will love alway.

> So cool I found the water
> I plunged into the spray;
> And underneath an oak tree
> In the cool freshness lay.
> > A long time have I loved you,
> > And I will love alway.

On she sang, sometimes her voice so low he could barely catch the words. But finally, coming to the last stanza, the tones came soft and clear as a little bell:

> I wish the cruel roses
> In the dark ocean lay,
> That I and my dear sweetheart
> Might live in love for aye.
> > A long time have I loved you,
> > And I will love alway.

She ceased, swept the accumulated rubbish into the fireplace, put the broom in its corner, and picking up the two birch bark pails, opened the door, passed out, and went to the spring to refill them.

David Cameron sat and gazed at the flames leaping up the broad chimney. The sweet sadness of her voice when she had sung the last stanza of the song had strangely disturbed him.

He remembered—yes, he would remember as long as he lived—the touch of her lips on his cheek the night his fever had changed for the better. Of course she had been under a great physical and mental strain; never sparing herself during her father's illness, and now overwrought by his own.

Had it merely been the impulsive, sisterly act of a warm-hearted girl, deeply grateful that the man she was convinced had saved her father's life, was now out of danger? It would seem so. She never once now called him P'sazum, or even David. It was "Monsieur Cameron" always. She continued to wait on him with kindness and solicitude, to bring him food, to plump his pillow of moss and turn it over. When finally he had been allowed to get up for a short time each day, she had put on his stockings and shoes; and when she thought he had been up long enough, gently but firmly ordered him back to his bunk. But withal he thought there was a studied aloofness in her manner, as though she were determined to banish from his mind the fact that—for whatever reason—she had momentarily overstepped the bounds of maidenly modesty.

So David sat there in the little cabin of Raoul Chartier, his brain in a muddle, not knowing what to think of Jeanne's marked change of attitude towards him. It couldn't go on like this, he told himself: the very air filled with his knowledge that a barrier had been raised between them.

Finally he got to his feet, walked slowly to the little window, facing the river and the opposite hills, and gazed at the galaxy of colour that cloaked the maple and elm trees.

Scarlet were the maples, and purple; and some were all golden, as were many of the elms. And where the sun fell on them they glistened like leaf-gold that has newly come from the rollers of a goldsmith. And the colours were reflected on the placid surface of the river, and on the ripples made by the bar where the Medaweska meets the larger water of the Wul-ahs-tukw.

The door opened. The girl entered and set her buckets of water on the bench beside the door. And turning, seeing him standing by the window, she said in a reproving voice, "Monsieur Cameron is not yet strong enough to stand."

"I was looking at the trees. They are very lovely," he said.

"Yes," and she nodded. "I saw them. But now Monsieur Cameron must go back to his chair. Indeed, it is again time he is in the bed."

"Oh," he demurred, "not yet, Mademoiselle, I will sit a little longer. I shall never get strong, if I lie on my back so much." And walking to his chair he seated himself.

There was silence for a little while. The girl was busy at the table, singing anew the last stanza of *A la Claire Fontaine*, but in tones so low he could barely catch the words:

> I wish the cruel roses
> In the dark ocean lay,
> That I and my dear sweetheart
> Might live in love for aye.
>> A long time have I loved you,
>> And I will love alway.

When she had ended the refrain he said:

"Jeanne, Mademoiselle, will you kindly sit down so that I may talk to you?"

"Yes, Monsieur." She came and seated herself on the bench beside the fire, opposite him. "You see," she said smiling, "Monsieur has but to command, and his maidservant obeys. Yes, Monsieur?"

"It was not a command, Mademoiselle. At least I hope not. For I would not be thought discourteous."

The smile vanished from her lips. "I beg Monsieur's pardon. I was—what do you call it?—making play. One cannot always be serious. It is not good. One must make play some times. And Monsieur is so serious…much more than when he came. We French, we laugh much, even when sometimes we do not feel like laughing."

"Oh," he said soberly, "am I then always so serious?" And added, more to himself than to her: "We Scots are said to be a dour race."

"But, yes, much of the time, and Monsieur is so closed up with his thoughts, and that is not good. Perhaps it is because Monsieur has been ill, that he is so changed, so closed up. Do you suppose, Monsieur, that that would be it?"

"I did not realize I was changed," he said. "I am sorry, Mademoiselle." He laughed a trifle nervously, was silent a few moments, wondering if he could ever say what was clamouring for utterance.

She was speaking. "I crave Monsieur's pardon. It is unfortunate the conversation took a turn that was not meant at the beginning. Is it not so, Monsieur Cameron?"

He nodded, "Yes, Mademoiselle, that is so; but conversation often takes such turns. What I started to say is, that…I have a complaint to make and…a confession." He paused.

She had been leaning towards him, an eager look in her hazel eyes that now swiftly changed to one of frank dismay. She said:

"Yes, Monsieur? Start at the beginning, please."

He went on, his manner distrait. "Mademoiselle has been so… so formal of late. I mean since I began to get well. She has never once called me *P'sazum*, or *Monsieur David*, always *Monsieur*! Have I said or done anything unkind?"

For a few moments she seemed confused. Finally, "No, Monsieur has always been most courteous. And now, will Monsieur please continue?"

"But Mademoiselle has not given me a reason for her sudden formality," he protested.

She laughed lightly. "Monsieur is so persistent. Well, I will hear what he has to confess, then I may be able to answer him more fully. Yes…?"

He took a deep breath. "I told you a falsehood," he began, and paused.

"Oh?" she murmured, with raised eyebrows.

"Yes, Mademoiselle. That night when the fever changed—I told you I dreamt that you had kissed me. But I *knew* it was *not* a dream."

She flushed crimson. Then hastily, "It is not fair for Monsieur to remind me, even to make excuse for his falsehood. It was a weakness, a momentary weakness; but if Monsieur is satisfied by reminding me of a now most regrettable incident, it is enough."

If she had struck him he would not have been more hurt.

He was silent a few moments, then said, "I am very sorry, Mademoiselle, I meant it not that way. I have been a blundering donkey. What I have been trying to say is, that what you did had caused me to hope I could say what is in my heart, and it would be acceptable to you. Now I know differently: that it was a regrettable incident. I can only ask Mademoiselle's forgiveness for my presumption in thinking that the miracle—your token of sisterly affection, shall I say?—meant any more than that. But I want you to know, Mademoiselle, that when I leave, which will be just as soon as I am able to travel, I will carry back with me memories of you as beautiful as they are sad." He paused again, brushed a hand across his brow in a helpless gesture.

She sprang to her feet and was beside him with one swift movement. "Oh, Monsieur," she cried, "forgive me. I have been unkind. But it was not my heart that was speaking. For while your words were innocent of any intention to be unkind, mine were meant to hurt, and I said what was not true." She paused, timidly reached down and touched his hand. Then she went on: "I too, would remember the beautiful things." She paused again, and, her voice little above a whisper: "I shall have to help you, *P'sazum, Kul-a-waz-oo P'sazum.* Tell me, what is it you would say that is in your heart?"

Now with a rush of words he spoke. And he was like a little boy as he said, "It is this, Jeanne: I love you. I have loved you ever since that far day I saw you in the little chapel at Medowktek. That is why I came all the leagues up the river. It was one of my reasons for again coming to Acadia. I tried to tell you that day by the waterfall. But when I asked you if you loved any one, you said yes, but that you were not promised to wed. And oh, my dear, I thought it was some officer of Boishébert's garrison, or possibly someone you had met at Quebec. And you said it was neither one nor the other. Then you jumped up and told me it was your wish that I leave Medaweska. Do you remember, Jeanne?" He paused, and she said:

"I remember, P'sazum. It was the day the little bird sang: 'T*i-ne-li-ain-Nicolai-Nicolai-Denys-Denys.*' You were so blind not to guess the truth—that it was you I loved. But it is now a deeper love, and it will never die, my dear. Oh, David, you have been such a long, long time telling me." She paused, dropped to her knees beside him and hid her face against his jacket.

He put his arms about her, held her yet closer, and bending, pressed his lips to the hair that curled in chestnut waves from beneath her little linen cap, around the edge of which were embroidered flowers alternately red and blue, and murmured her name over and over.

Then she lifted her face, and he saw that her eyes were filled with tears. And they ran down her cheeks, fell to her white collar, and from thence found refuge on her brown woollen bodice. Now she said:

"Yes, P'sazum, I ran from you. But even as I ran my heart wanted me to stay. Oh, I was quite shameless! I wanted to hear you say you loved me, even while I was afraid Etienne would do you injury. But yes, even while I told you to leave Medaweska, I tried to will you to stay. Oh, my dear, my dear, I thought you were so stupid, so blind, not to know the truth. But now let me tell you, that this failure of yours to know how lovable you are, makes you the more dear to me.

"And I thought too, how can he love me? He is rich in this world's goods, while we have lost all. You have seen our poverty— that we are little better off than the poor Indians. Besides, there must be so many beautiful women in your own country."

At this he gently put his hand over her lips. "Hush," he said. "As for poverty, my dear, were it not that I have plans to help your Acadian people, I would be willing to send word to the captain of my ship to take her home, and I would gladly stay here. For where love is, there is home, and nothing else matters.

"As for other women, Jeanne—yes, there are many lovely women in my own country, but none more fair than you, my dear."

She flushed with pleasure, and drying her eyes, reached up, and cupping his face in her two hands, her lips sought his.

Presently, she leaned back, and her eyes were troubled as she said, "And there is our religion…" She paused, shook her head as though *that* were a barrier final and insurmountable.

"Listen, my dear," he said earnestly, "all religions are the outgrowth of one that stretches back into primitive ages. In other words, men of all races have acknowledged a divine creator. Our North American Indians believed this. They recognized the good principle, and the bad principle, and that justice would be meted out according to man's acts.

"When Tomah and I made our escape from slavery in Virginia, we often knelt in the wilderness and prayed; he in his way, I in mine. More often he said a little prayer taught him by the Fathers at Medowktek. But sometimes I have seen him walk to a growing tree, and make a little slit in the bark with his knife or tomahawk. Then he put his forefinger to his lips, and moistening it with his tongue, he touched it to the exposed inner skin of the tree; which done, he reverently pressed the two edges of the bark together.

"Then in my childish curiosity I said to him, 'What do you do, Tomah?' And he answered me thus: 'Tomah says a prayer to the Great Spirit in the old, old time way, before Fathers came to the river. Tell Him thanks with the life that is on the lips, and in the tongue. *Ah-ha*, maybe He hear better, if we tell Him both ways.'

"And, my dear, I at first thought it a heathen practice; but after I had grown to young manhood, remembering what he had done, I said to myself, 'Who can be heathen who prays to God with his heart, be it one way or another?'"

She smiled up at him, her lovely eyes alight with understanding. He continued:

"It was the same later in the little Maliseet chapel at Medowktek. Although not a Catholic, I often entered it and prayed. Not that I believe God is confined within four walls; for he is everywhere, but because the place had been dedicated to Him, and many had prayed there; and I had been taught to go to church.

"Since then, I have travelled much. I visited the country of the Turks, and India, and Spain, and Portugal. I have knelt and prayed with devout Mohammedans, and in cathedrals of the old world, and at simple wayside shrines. And once, journeying in the Arabian desert with the wild Bedouins, I knelt in the sand when they knelt at morning and evening, and while they prayed to Allah, the one God, I too prayed. For God is God by whichever name he is called.

"I will not say that I could ever bring myself to forsake the particular belief of my father; and no more do I expect any man to change *his* belief for mine. For his is to him just as pure and holy as is mine to me." He paused a moment, his eyes fixed on her upturned face, then added, "Do you understand, my dear, that any religious differences need not stand between us?"

She nodded, "When you talk like this, everything seems so simple. But I doubt not the good priest could advance reasons that to him are just as valid why we should not wed."

"But you *will* marry me?" he added anxiously.

"Yes, P'sazum; because my heart is now sure that it is right. I was afraid you would want me to conform to your particular creed. And for me to do that would be a negation of *my* belief; I would have violated my soul's integrity, and it would die."

"You are right," he said. "And you are as good and wise as you are beautiful. With your permission, I will at the first opportunity speak to Father Germain."

"Do so," she said eagerly. "But I too must tell him; I have *much* to tell him."

"I must also talk to your father, Jeanne, I—" He was about to add that he should have done so when he first came, but she broke in with:

"That is right too." Then demurely, "He already knows. I told him I loved you that first day after you returned from the hunt."

"And what was his answer, Jeanne dear?"

She smiled softly, then said, "He told me that my happiness was his. He added, 'Monsieur will make you a good husband. And so, my little one, if he asks you, say yes. It is my wish.'" She paused, then went on, "I am always his *little* Jeanne to him. But, my dear, I am not so *very little*, am I? I am to your shoulder."

He smiled, and, remembering what Tomah had said on the way hither:

"The Chief assured me you would be just a little above it; and Tomah has an accurate eye."

Now she rose with haste, and taking David's arm, said with gentle firmness:

"Come, my dear, you have been up too long; you must lie down, and I will bring you some of the good broth with meat in it. And you shall eat a corn bread also, so that you may grow strong again." And she led him to his bunk, and tucked the blankets about him. Then with a kiss she left him, hastened to the fireplace, where she put on more wood, and hung the skillet on the iron crane. As she moved from place to place her moccasined feet made only little brushing sounds on the floor, like those of a fawn deer walking through dry leaves.

Presently she began to sing, low and sweet, like a contented housewife:

> Sainte Marguerite,
> Veillez ma petite!
> > Endormez ma p'tite enfant
> > Jusqu'à l'age de quinze ans!
> > Quand elle aura quinze ans passé,
> > Il faudra la marier,
> > Avec un p'tit bonhomme
> > Qui viendra de Rome.

> (Saint Marguerite in thy keeping
> I leave my baby sleeping!
> > Lull to sleep my little one
> > Until fifteen years have gone;
> > When has passed her fifteenth year

Send to her a Cavalier,
Who will take her home
To the great City of Rome.)

And listening, David Cameron was happier than he had been for many a long year. He closed his eyes. Presently the door opened. It was Tomah. He stood his gun in a corner, slipped his powder horn and bag of bullets from his shoulders, hung them on a peg, and coming to David's side, he said in Maliseet:

"As Tomah walked over the ridge, he came to a spring of water, at the base of a great birch tree. There was green moss all around it; and Tomah knelt in the moss to drink, for he had walked a long, long distance; and as he bent his mouth to drink, he saw two faces looking up from the water, that was as clear as my son's little glass he shaves by. And one was my son's face, and the other was that of the *P'l-etch-e-min* maid. And they both smiled up at me. *Ah-ha,* they looked happy. Tomah knew she made promise to be my son's woman. *Ah-ha,* it was *me-ta-o-lin.*"

Now the Chief walked over to the fireplace, and taking out his pipe and tobacco, both of which he always carried about his neck in a small pursed bag of tanned deer skin, he filled and lighted his pipe. Then he sat down cross-legged on the floor beside the fire. He sat immobile, like a statue, his dark eyes and tawny face as tranquil as the waters of a windless lake.

41

By the second week of October the leaves of the maples, beeches, birches and elms had all fallen. They covered the ground beneath with russet, purple, red and gold. Night sprinkled them with frost—which some call stardust. But when day came, the sun dispersed it, and drank up the moisture, so that the air was filled with a subtle odour, a witching incense that is only compounded by Nature, from whom no secret of alchemy has been withheld since the dawn of time.

Two days before the wedding ceremony of Jeanne Chartier and David Cameron, Etienne d'Amours came first to one, then the other. And to Jeanne he said simply:

"You will forgive me, Mademoiselle Jeanne, that I feel it necessary to leave before the event; but the good Father has urgent need for a message to be taken to Monsignor, the Bishop at Quebec. Each day now is important, for one never knows when the ice will close the small rivers, or snow fill in the portages." He paused, thrust a hand into his pocket, and brought out a little box fashioned out of winter birch bark, and sewed with tiny peeled spruce roots. In size it was exactly two and a half inches by one and three-eighths. He held it out to her.

"It is my wedding gift to you," he said. "Treasure it; it is very old, and very precious to me, Mademoiselle Jeanne."

Tears sprang to her eyes. For she knew that the box contained the little silver reliquary, its cover incised with the figure of Christ, that had been the cherished possession of his great grandmother, wife of that Mathieu d'Amours, and mother of the four sons whose seigniorial grants in Acadia had once included all the land on the Wul-ahs-tukw, between the Ah-jem-sec and the falls of Chic-seen-i-beg.

175

She took it in the palm of her left hand and protectingly covered it with her right, as when one had captured a small bird and wants to quieten its fear. And she said, her voice low with emotion, "I will always treasure it, and remember you, Etienne." Then, reaching up, she kissed him on the cheek.

His dark face flushed; she saw he was trembling. But he said huskily:

"And I shall always treasure your kiss, Mademoiselle. I shall remember it when I push my canoe up the rivers; and when I find my way through the forests, I shall feel it on my cheek."

Then Etienne came to David and spoke privately. After repeating that he must leave for Quebec with a message from the priest, he added:

"Monsieur knows with what hatred and suspicion I at first regarded him. That is past. It was past when you saved my life. I love Mademoiselle Chartier. But even had you not come, she never would have wed me. I am happy then that it is you. I know you will be kind to her. I will often pray good Saint Ann to intercede for your safe passage to your own country, and after." He paused, and seizing David's hand, gave it a pressure that almost made the Scot wince. Then releasing it, he said, his strong voice husky, "Adieu, Monsieur David."

A little later he walked to the river where his canoe was already loaded for his journey. Lifting it into the water, he picked up his setting pole, stepped in, and pushed off on his long journey to Quebec.

David and Jeanne stood watching him pole along the shore water. Just before reaching the Medaweska, they saw him half turn, glance back, and momentarily lift one hand from his setting pole to wave a final farewell. Then, meeting the onrush of the cross-current, he pushed the stern far outward, got his canoe straight, and passed slowly from view.

They knew the reason for Etienne's hurried departure, and felt it was better so, for his own sake, and did not blame him.

42

It was a beautiful windless morning on which they were married. The ceremony was performed a few rods from Raoul Chartier's cabin, beneath the huge pine tree that reared its height in patriarchal splendour above all others in the valley. Near its base the priest had erected a little lectern. It had been carefully hewed by Tomah from a section cut from a black-ash tree. But the Chief told only David why he chose the ash: because it is *me-ta-o-lin* (magic). For it was into this tree that Glooskap, the Maliseet divinity of old time, had shot arrows and peopled the east-land with men of his race.

David Cameron has described in simple and eloquent words how his bride looked that day: She wore her brown woollen dress, it being all she possessed; although she could not have looked more lovely in the richest wedding gown. Over the tight-fitting bodice the white linen collar fell almost to her shoulders. Her feet were shod in low, moosehide moccasins, decorated with beads and dyed porcupine quills; for indeed she had no other footwear; the shoes she had been wearing when she fled up the river from St. Ann's were long since worn out. And from beneath her little linen cap her hair hung in long twin braids. Her face, eyes, everything about her was lovely; not only with a physical loveliness, but with something spiritual that transcends all these, and without which a woman's beauty is no deeper than the colour of her cheeks. And although more than fifty years have passed since that day, he still sees in her this spiritual radiancy, which is the essence of all real beauty, and which has no end.

So David Cameron and Jeanne Chartier were made man and wife, the ring used being that which Monsieur Chartier had given to her mother on *their* wedding day. And when the formalities subsequent to such affairs had been complied with, they and all the inhabitants of Medaweska partook of a wedding feast. Two of the hunters had shot wild ducks; others brought partridges, which with moose meat were roasted on spits before an open fire. For wedding cake Madame Cormier had baked a great loaf of corn-meal, since they had no white flour. Into this she had put many of the little beech nuts the children had found among the leaves on the slopes of the ridge, whither they had fallen when they slipped their frail moorings from the mother tree. And the flavour of these tiny nuts is superior to that of all the fruits of Araby. And she had sweetened the cake with syrup made from the sap of the maple, and dusted over it maple sugar, shaved from a precious lump she had been hoarding for the celebration of the Nativity, which includes a feast after the singing of the old time Noëls.

And when it was all over, and everybody had kissed everybody else, and the women had wept a little, and the farewells had been said, the bride and the groom, and Jeanne's father, accompanied by all the inhabitants of Medaweska, went to the river, where Tomah's canoe, newly pitched, awaited them.

It was lifted into the water, and while the Chief steadied it, David took his wife's hand as she got in and seated herself in the seat made of basket ash, the back resting against the middle cross bar. Then her father—who was going with them to Scotland—got into the bow seat, and David behind Jeanne.

The Chief picked up his paddle, stepped in and pushed off. Reaching deeper water, he sank to his knees with the sure, flowing movement of a cat. Now he swung the canoe farther out, where the current is stronger, his paddle blade slicing into the water with the silence of an otter, to sweep sternwards, and then, withdrawn, repeat its rhythmic movements.

43

Thus they left Medaweska. Before reaching the bend of the river Jeanne turned her head and looked back at the little crowd who still stood watching the canoe. They would stand so until it had passed from view. Tears dimmed her eyes. They were her own people. Together they had dared innumerable dangers, and, fleeing to this refuge of hope, had laboured together with song and jest to rear their rude habitations out of the primeval wilderness. But she now knew that on his return to his native country, this man she had wedded would, in his own determined way, see to it that her people were accorded the privilege of domicile in this land of Acadia, which they loved with the simple and abiding devotion that is a dominant characteristic of the race.

She lifted her hand high above her head in final farewell, and, turning, bravely winked the tears from her eyes. Then, as she felt David's hand gently patting her shoulder, she said:

"It is all right, my dear. It is only natural to weep a little."

A few minutes later she began to sing, in a low voice the *Jesus Ahatonhia*:

> 'Twas in the moon of winter time when all the birds had fled,
> That mighty Gitchie Manitou sent angel choirs instead.
> Before their light the stars grew dim,
> And wand'ring hunters heard the hymn;
> Jesus, your king, is born; Jesus is born; in excelsis gloria!
>
> Within a lodge of broken bark the tender babe was found.
> A ragged robe of rabbit skin enwrapped his beauty round.
> And as the hunter braves drew nigh,

The angel song sang loud and high:
Jesus, your king, is born; Jesus is born; in excelsis gloria!

The earliest moon of winter time is not so round and fair
As with the ring of glory on the helpless infant there.
While Chiefs from far above him knelt,
With gifts of fox and beaver pelt.
Jesus, your king, is born; Jesus is born; in excelsis gloria!

O Children of the forest free, O sons of Manitou,
The Holy Child of earth and heav'n is born today for you.
Come, kneel before the radiant boy
Who brings you beauty, peace and joy.
Jesus, your king, is born; Jesus is born; in excelsis gloria!

When she had ended she turned her head and said to David:

"It is a very, very old Noël I heard at the convent. The good Sister who sang it told me it was written by the sainted martyr, Jean Brébeuf, for the Huron Indians. Is it not beautiful, my dear? And how I love the line: 'A ragged robe of rabbit skin enwrapped His beauty round'; and, again, 'while Chiefs from far before Him knelt, with gifts of fox and beaver pelt.' It is so precious. Is it not so, David?"

He nodded, enraptured as well by the sound of her voice as the words of the Noël. "Some day," he said, "I must try to translate it into Maliseet for Tomah and his people."

They reached the camp site above the falls of Chic-seen-i-beg two hours before dark, where, after eating, they made a small wigwam for the use of David and Jeanne, covering the floor a foot deep with small fir boughs. Then a like mattress was laid beneath the canoe, under which Tomah and Raoul Chartier were to sleep.

When night closed in they sat about the campfire and talked. And it was here that Monsieur Chartier suggested it would perhaps be wise if, on their arrival at Medowktek, he were to take a separate route to the sea, in order to escape possible detention by English scouts or soldiery on the lower reaches of the river.

"As you know, David," he added, "our people are still being hunted and, whenever found, subjected to indignities and exile."

"Ah," said David, "but you are now my father-in-law, and any arrest would only be temporary."

"Even a temporary detention would be embarrassing for everyone concerned," objected Monsieur Chartier. "With Jeanne it is different. She is now your wife. That makes everything all right. And so, my son, if you will pick me up at Passamaquoddy, I will go there by way of the St. Croix waters. As you know, the Indians of that place are blood kin to the Maliseets, speaking the same language. Many of them have traded with me, and will welcome my sojourn among them until you arrive."

And so it was agreed. Then David asked Tomah to tell the old legend about the Maliseet maiden Malibeam, whose splendid sacrifice saved the lives of her people from death by the Mohawks.

So Tomah began, and his telling it was the same, save for some slight variations, that David had heard from the lips of Moxus fourteen years before, as they camped at this place during their journey from Quebec to their Maliseet village at Medowktek.

Said Tomah:

"Malibeam she was a brave Maliseet *Nuk-sqa* (girl). She lived a long, long time ago, before the white man came to Acadia. She stayed at the mouth of the Medaweska with her father and four, five brothers. One year when it was the time of the hunters' moon, Malibeam she stay in the wigwam and make baskets. Father and brothers they go down river, below Chic-seen-i-beg, to hunt moose. They be gone for five, six days. One day after they had gone, four canoes filled with Mohawk warriors came to the mouth of the Medaweska where Malibeam stay in wigwam and make baskets. They take her prisoner, and say: 'Where your people?' and she say they down river two days' journey. Then the Chief he say he set her free if she take them to where they make camp. And she say: 'All right, but I go in my own canoe.' She have little canoe eight, nine foot long.

"It was afternoon when they start. But it dark long time, and they not come to Chic-seen-i-beg. Bye and bye Chief say to Malibeam: 'How far now?' And she say: 'Not so far—might be two, three mile.'

Well, they go on; Malibeam she go ahead. Bye and bye the Chief say: 'What that noise? Sound like falls.' And Malibeam she say: 'Ah-ha, that Chic-seen-i-beg. He make big noise. But bye and bye we go to shore and portage round him.' And she paddle fast. All the time sound of falls get bigger; and bye and bye Chief say: 'Must be time go to shore and make portage,' but Malibeam say: 'No, not yet. Plenty time for that.' But Chief hard to hear Malibeam, because that Chic-seen-i-beg now make such big roar.

"Bye and bye water she get so swift canoes go like arrow. Then moon come up, and Chief and other men in canoes see great wall high in air, like smoke; and Chic-seen-i-beg roar louder. Then they know Malibeam play them trick. They try to paddle for shore; but water so swift only one canoe able to reach it. They pull up canoe quick. They look, and they see Malibeam in her little canoe go into the smoke wall that is the breath of Chic-seen-i-beg when he mad. And Malibeam's voice come to them above sound of falls, clear, like the bell in the chapel at Medowktek: 'My people—I save my people!' She stand out in the moonlight like big flame. Then she gone. Mohawk canoes they go too. Chic-seen-i-beg take them.

"Mohawks that make shore go back to their own country and tell the story about Malibeam. *Ah-ha*, that how all Indians in the east-land know what she do."

Tomah's voice ceased. And David felt Jeanne's hand creep into his, like some small thing that seeks sanctuary from storm or danger. And David held her hand close, and broke the silence, thanking Tomah; telling him that it could not be better told by any raconteur in all the world.

44

They were up at daybreak. Soon after breakfast the journey was resumed. From now on, save where it was necessary for Tomah to use his setting pole to drop through some rock-strewn rapids, Monsieur Chartier and David alternately used the bow paddle. For they had yet some two hundred miles to go before reaching the river's mouth. And since the days were now much shorter, and the nights colder, for Jeanne's greater comfort David was anxious to reach the Bay as soon as possible. Therefore, when they saw Indians on shore, they stopped not; merely giving a wave of the paddles in greeting.

Reaching Medowktek they paused only to eat and pitch the seams of the canoe. Here Monsieur Chartier secured the services of Pemmyhawick and Peter Loler to take him by way of the Eel River waters to Passamaquoddy. They set off at once, for it was a three days' journey. David purchased a rug made of lucivee[§] skins for Jeanne should she become cold at any time on the journey. Now he said his final farewell to Tomah's squaw, and to all those who had not yet departed on the winter's hunt; and then embarking, they sped down river.

Twelve miles below Medowktek the river flows dark and deep between shores covered with huge granite boulders, with the current finally swinging sharply to the left. David, who was in the bow, saw that a couple of hundred yards ahead of them there was a sudden drop in the bed of the river, over which the accumulated water from above rushed like a mill race. Farther down, almost a quarter mile, a wall of water, its crest white with foam, spread diagonally half-way across the river. Knowing that this was the Sheogomoc Rapids, he turned and looked apprehensively at Tomah.

The Chief nodded composedly, and swung the canoe close to the shore in a few inches of water. Getting out he grasped the gunwale. "Sheogomoc he bad," he said in English. "Sometimes canoe take in water. Might wet your woman. Better walk on shore. It is safe. Tomah will run canoe through alone, then come back and carry baggage."

David stepped to the shore, then helped Jeanne out. The baggage was unloaded. Then Tomah placed two granite rocks, which would weigh fifty pounds, in the bow of his canoe.

David took Jeanne's hand, "Come, my dear," he said, "we will find a good spot to watch him."

Together they hastened along the rocky shore, and coming to a great flat-topped boulder of granite, David jumped up on it and helped Jeanne up beside him. "We can now see everything," he told her.

She smiled at him. "I do wish I had been allowed to go through with Tomah."

"Too dangerous, Jeanne. Look—there he goes!"

They saw Tomah shoot by them like an arrow. He was standing a little ahead of the stern, his shoulders slightly stooped as he swung his paddle with strong, steady strokes. The canoe lifted with the swell, flattened out, lifted again, the water racing along its sides.

They saw it near the wall of water. Now Tomah sank to his knees. He swung the bow a little to the right, so that the swell would take the canoe on its quarter.

The light craft pitched forward, half buried its nose in the wall of water. Now it rose until the whole side of the bottom was momentarily visible from bow to stern; then it slid over the crest. For a brief second it was lost to view, then they saw it, shooting like a rocket in a diagonal course towards the left hand shore.

David breathed a sigh of relief. Jeanne clapped her hands. Her eyes were shining. "I still wish I had gone through with him."

He smiled at her and shook his head. "You are too precious to trust even to Tomah's care. Ah, the Chief has landed, is coming back for the baggage."

A half hour later they were again on the way, and made camp that night at an old camping place opposite an island that Tomah said was called Quoac.

By next day they reached Ek-pa-hawk, but passed on quickly; for they did not want to stop and make conversation with the Indians there.

On they went, league upon league. When Jeanne was tired of sitting up, she stretched out upon a bed of blankets they had made for her on the floor of the canoe.

And sometimes the gentle sway of the canoe, the rhythmic dip of the paddles, and the water purling along the gunwales lulled her to sleep, as a child is sleepened by the rocking of a cradle.

Three days from Medowktek it began to rain, and continued without letup for two days and nights. They hastily constructed a wigwam of birch bark, overlapping the sheets so that no drops could enter. Then they collected wood, and, making a fire just outside the little opening left for the doorway, kept it going day and night until the rain ceased.

The enforced lay-up was hard on their store of provisions, and they would have fared ill, had it not been that a flock of black ducks alighted on the water within easy musket range. Tomah and David charged their guns with small-shot, and firing, killed half a dozen of them.

When at length it ceased raining, they again set off. They had gone but a little distance when Jeanne pointed ahead to the left hand shore, and said to David: "There, my dear, is the Ah-jem-sec river. My mother is buried there. May we stop, please?"

David spoke to Tomah, who swung the canoe shorewards. Having landed, and while Tomah remained with the canoe, Jeanne and David clambered up the bank, and side by side walked towards the dilapidated fort and buildings. As they approached nearer, a porcupine, which the Indians call *Mod-i-wess*, came from the gateway and ambled unconcernedly away.

They did not enter the fort, but passed to the right of it, where finally, coming to a little mound with a flat stone lying upon it, they stopped. Neither spoke for several moments. Presently Jeanne bent, and, picking up a bit of moss, brushed off the sand and leaves covering most of the letters that announced that here rested the mortal remains of Madame Jeanne Anastasie Chartier, who died June 23rd, 1751.

Now the girl knelt, David beside her. And he could hear her whispered prayer for the soul of the dead. Then, rising from their knees, and crossing herself, Jeanne said: "It seems so…alone, here in the wilderness. And yet," she added, "she knew much happiness in this place, and I am sure it is where she would want to be." With a last look at the grave she wiped the tears from her eyes, and taking David's arm they retraced their steps to the river.

A little later, as the canoe sped over the choppy waves, Jeanne said to David, "As I have told you before, my life at Ah-jem-sec had its happy side. Often I went with the Indians in their canoes far up the Ah-jem-sec, which is a very pleasant, quiet river, to where it empties from a great lake many leagues long and more than a league wide. There were ducks there in abundance.

"Then, as you know, when I was twelve, my father took me to the seminary at Quebec. It was then that I first saw you, my dear. But little did I imagine that ever I should see you again, or that I should be your own dear wife."

"Ah, said he," but did you not think sometimes of me?"

"Yes, David. In fancy I could see you standing on the high bank near the Medowktek fort, looking down at us in the canoe. And you looked so sad, so forlorn. And I often wondered if the lad that was you had ever reached his own land.

"Finally," she went on, "my memory of you grew dim; for you must know there were many other girls my own age, as well as older, at the seminary; and we had various activities. And then, after four years, my father brought me back to Acadia, by the same route we had gone to Quebec. We stopped a few hours at Medowktek; and there my father made enquiries, and learned that you had departed from the village a year after I saw you." She paused, and with a low tinkle of laughter continued:

"Tomah was not there, and it was another Indian who said, '*Ah-ha*, the little English with the hair that is the colour of *Gwaksus* (the red fox) has gone'." She turned and smiled at him.

He laughed. "I am quite conscious of my hair. When I was a boy at school, my companions called me 'Red Cameron'."

"I love it," she said. "Almost anyone can have black hair, or fair hair, but only few can have hair like yours, that is an alloy of copper and brass: what do you call it?— Ah, bronze, that is it."

45

They went forty miles that day—having passed, without stopping, the place where the vanguard of New Englanders had surveyed lots for their settlement—camped for the night, had a good sleep, and rose at daybreak. Tomah said they were now but ten miles from the river's mouth and should make it in two hours at most.

It was a fair day. The sun struck gleaming facets from the little waves, where flocks of white gulls, like miniature argosies, tacked this way and that from trough to swell.

The river was now much wider, the granite hills higher, and covered with spruce, fir, and pine, intermixed with hardwoods. The air was filled with the sweet, tangy odour of the sea.

The current too became swifter—a dark, impetuous flood hurrying to discharge itself through the towering quartzite palisades below.

It is said, that in times past a great tree, its roots wedged in some hidden cleft of rock, reared its polished crest tantalus-like, a dozen feet above the surface of the waters, and that the Indians, deeming it to possess powers of evil, had shot many of their best arrows at it; not in the hope of destroying it, but as offerings meant to propitiate its malefic nature.

This, in essence, is what Tomah told David and Jeanne, as he steered his canoe towards the cove above the falls.

Reaching it, they landed and unloaded the canoe. Then, shouldering their baggage, and with Tomah in the lead, they took the portage path that led around the falls to the harbour below.

Jeanne kept close to David. Finally she said, "My dear, are you quite, quite sure that the commandant of the fort will not take me and send me to Halifax, as he did the Acadian who came from Quebec?"

David chuckled. "No, Jeanne; you have nothing to fear, now that you are my wife, and are with *me*."

"Ah," she said, "but if on the way soldiers should intercept us, they might take me in spite of you and Tomah." And she edged a little closer to him.

And he repeated, "You are now my wife. You are a Scot!"

"Oh no, my dear," she protested quickly, "though I love you, and am your own dear wife, I am *not* a Scot. Indeed, I am French, and I would not say otherwise." And she said it with such sweet earnestness that he said:

"My dear, if it were possible for me to do so, I would love you more for having said that. But it will not be necessary for you to make any report to his soldiers, or the commandant of the Fort. In a very little while we shall be on board my ship. Then I shall visit the commandant, Colonel Arbuthnot, at the fort; for I have much to say to him concerning the Indians and your people."

"Oh," she said, "you will not leave me, David?" and her dismay was so real that he assured her:

"You will be as safe on board my ship as you will be in our home in Aberdeen. But, dear heart, if it will make you feel safer, I will leave Tomah with you until I have returned."

"And he will have his gun loaded?" she asked.

"Yes," he answered, "and the crew of my ship would fight for you too, if it were necessary. But it will not be necessary."

She gave him a sweet smile. "Then," she said, "I shall have no more of fear." And walked blithely beside him along the portage, that had been worn by the moccasined feet of countless aborigines long before the white man had seen the shores of Acadia.

As Jeanne walked beside her husband over this old trail, she unfolded a little of the story that has survived, about the taking of the fort of Charles la Tour by his rival d'Aulnay Charnisay.

"It is a long story," she said. "It was told to me by my mother, who had it from *her* mother, to whom it was related by Nicolas Denys. I shall only tell a little now. You must know, my dear, that Monsieur la Tour's rival—Charnisay—lived at Port Royal, across the Great Bay. And Charnisay claimed all of la Tour's land, over which he had been given jurisdiction by the king. And one day while la Tour was absent in France—leaving his wife Marie in charge of the Fort—Charnisay came with two or three armed ships and attempted to take it. But he was met with such discharges of cannon, and his ship was so severely damaged that he was obliged to withdraw. But in two months he returned, and bringing his ships in close, called on the garrison to surrender. He was answered by shouts of defiance and volleys of cannon shot and small arms.

"For three days Madame la Tour inspired her little garrison with her own indomitable courage, and fought off the besiegers, and again crippled them so that they were forced to retire out of reach of the guns.

"But on the fourth day the enemy landed unobserved, and while many of the garrison slept, a miserable Swiss sentinel, seeing them, failed to give the alarm. They were already placing scaling ladders against the walls and mounting them when others of the garrison awoke and sounded the call to arms.

"They were greatly outnumbered, but Lady la Tour rallied the defenders, armed herself with steel corslet and sword, and fought at their side. And she only surrendered when most of her men were dead or wounded, and upon condition that the living be spared.

"And what did this perfidious Charnisay do, after they had laid down their arms? He violated his plighted word; and while Madame la Tour was made to look on, all save one—who was spared on condition that he be the executioner—were hanged.

"It is said that she survived but a few days, dying of a broken heart, and that her body was buried in an unmarked grave a short distance from the fort she had so valiantly tried to save for her absent lord.

"But whenever brave deeds are recounted, I am sure that among them will be included the story of this Huguenot woman, whose loyalty to the cause of her husband is equal to anything that has come out of ancient Greece or Rome. Do you not think so, my dear?"

"Yes," he replied, "and thank you Jeanne; you have told it well."

She flushed with pleasure; but said, "I was only repeating what Nicolas Denys told my grandmother."

"Nevertheless," he said warmly, "you have retold it very well."

46

They had now reached a spot where they had an unobstructed view of the harbour. David paused and pointed to three vessels anchored some distance from the fort. "See, Jeanne," he said, "there she is! Ah, the bonny ship—the big one, Jeanne. You can see her name on the bow '*Sheila Grahme*'; and the figurehead—all gold paint. *Ah-ha*, I see that Captain Fortescue has kept the men busy since he returned from New England."

"You knew she would be waiting?" she asked. "Did you never once fear that she might have been wrecked when she sailed to Boston and New York to dispose of her cargo?"

He laughed. "Yes; once or twice. But knowing the ship, and knowing Fortescue, my fears quietened. Come, my dear."

And so, following Tomah, they went down the hill; and coming at last to the beach opposite the ship, David raised his voice in a loud: "Ahoy, *Sheila Grahme*, Ahoy!"

A dozen sailors rushed to the rail, followed by a tall man whom David recognized as his Captain. "Ahoy, Fortescue!" called David. "Send a boat!"

A few moments, and they saw it being lowered. The oars were manned and it raced for the shore.

Five minutes later, David, Jeanne and Tomah were safely on deck. Captain Fortescue stepped forward. There was a puzzled look in his eyes as they rested momentarily on Jeanne's face. Then he thrust out his hand and took David's. "Ah, man, man," he cried. "I could not think what had detained ye so long! Another few days and I had sent the long boat up river to see if ye were alive or dead."

"Thank you, Captain," said David. "And now, good friend, I want to introduce to you my wife." He touched Jeanne's arm and said to her in French; "My dear, this is Captain Fortescue, who is the master of my ship. He is a very old and dear friend."

Captain Fortescue had removed his hat. Jeanne stepped back a pace and made him a little curtsey, then straightening, held out to him her small hand.

The Captain took it, bowed gravely and kissed it. Then, turning to the crew clustered about, he said: "Men, this is Master David Cameron's wife." Whereat one and all: mate and bo'sun, carpenters, gunners, and sailors, doffed their caps, and with one accord raised three such cheers as the harbour had seldom heard.

Jeanne's face flushed with pleasure and her hazel eyes sparkled, for she knew they were doing her honour. Now, with a gesture in which sweetness and modesty and thankfulness commingled, she put her fingers to her lips and threw a kiss that included all of them—at which they broke into renewed cheers.

And when it was all over, David turned to Tomah. Taking him by the arm, he led him to Captain Fortescue, and his voice was filled with profound feeling as he said:

"Captain Fortescue, this is Tomah, the Maliseet Chief about whom I have told you so much, and whom I love as men do a fond parent."

Shifting his gun to his left hand, Tomah put out his right, and as the Captain grasped it and smiled, he said in English, "Tomah is happy his son has returned safe to his own people. It is good. There is nothing more to say."

Now David said to the Captain, "We have been on short rations for several days, and need food. As soon as the cook can prepare something, we will eat. In the meantime I shall take my wife to my cabin."

"I will give orders immediately," said Captain Fortescue.

Before leaving the deck, David spoke to Tomah. "My father," he said, "it is my wish, and that of my wife, that you stay on board until we are ready to sail. We will eat together in a little while."

"It will be as my son says," said Tomah simply. And walked off to look at the cannon, the muskets and cutlasses ranged about the masts; the wheel with its polished spokes; and the gold-painted figurehead on the bow—that in his own language he called "P'sazum's Totem."

David led his wife down the companionway; coming to the door of his cabin, he opened it and ushered her inside. For a few moments she stood in bewildered silence, her eyes sweeping over the polished mahogany panelling and tables, the bed with its heavy curtains of crimson velvet, the ruby-coloured hanging lamp. Finally, she looked up at David and said awesomely:

"And this is all *yours*, David?"

"Yes, my dear. Of course the ship belongs to me and my partner, Ian Grahme. But this is my own particular cabin."

Then she put her little hand on his arm and said, "It is difficult to understand that you could marry poor me, who have no dower to bring you." At which he put his arms about her, and drawing her close, told her that she was dower enough for him, her love being more precious than riches or aught else that earth held.

Now he showed her where toilet articles were kept; and saying he would leave her until she was ready, he went on deck and found Captain Fortescue, to whom in a few words he related his romantic wooing of Jeanne Chartier.

And Captain Fortescue said to him, "Ah, Davie man, she is a bonny lass. All the bachelors in Aberdeen will be envying ye. And the lasses…aye, there'll be sad hairts among them for the losing of yourself."

47

Later in the afternoon David Cameron and Captain Fortescue, accompanied by a couple of armed sailors, were rowed to the west side of the harbour, and having landed, proceeded to Fort Frederick.

Colonel Arbuthnot was expecting them, for David had sent word earlier that he had returned and would be pleased to call on him.

They were met at the gate by the commandant himself. He shook hands with David and Captain Fortescue, and told the former he was much pleased that he had returned safely.

He led them to his own quarters where he bade them be seated. Then, when he had poured wine from a decanter, he said:

"I must admit, Mr. Cameron, that your prolonged absence has been a matter of concern to me, as well as to Captain Fortescue; for as I told you when you first arrived, the Indians, despite a lasting treaty they signed at Halifax, and the fact that we have opened a truck house here to which they bring furs quite regularly, are in a very unsettled state."

David nodded. Colonel Arbuthnot went on, "Of course, Mr. Cameron, you doubtless know that they have signed treaties in the past, and broken them whenever it suited their purpose to do so."

"Yes," said David, "I am aware of such instances. But in many cases it has been due to acts of ill-faith by our people. I could quote you many such instances. At the present, one of their grievances is that their priest has been sent away. You must know, Colonel Arbuthnot, that having been Catholics for many years, they much miss the consolation of the church."

"Quite so. I can understand that," agreed Colonel Arbuthnot. "The fact is, their priest went to Quebec, and was detained there by the authorities because he had incited not only them, but the few

Acadian remaining on the river, to flout our decrees. However, as for the latter, they have been pretty well taken care of."

"That is quite obvious, Colonel Arbuthnot, to any one who has had the opportunity, as I have, of seeing their abandoned farms," said David dryly. Then he added, "Frankly, I am happy that you have brought up the subject, since that is one reason for my visit to you this afternoon." He paused, and the commandant said:

"It has been a most grievous business, Mr. Cameron; and I shall sleep better nights when I am quite rid of it. One does not enjoy seeing the sufferings of women and children. But allow me to refill your glass Mr. Cameron, and yours, Captain Fortescue." Then to David, "I have much enjoyed Captain Fortescue's company since he returned from New England. To a brother Scot, duty-bound in this uncivilized place, his news of the homeland has been refreshing. Pardon me, Mr. Cameron, please go on."

"You have admitted, Colonel Arbuthnot," said David, "that in the Indians you have a more difficult problem on your hands. I quite agree with you. They are a proud race. Every one of them thinks he is as good, or better, than an Englishman; because they judge of a man's worth by his knowledge of war, woodcraft, hunting, fishing and trapping." He paused to sip his wine, and Colonel Arbuthnot said:

"But they are now a subject race, a defeated people. They—"

"Pardon me," interjected David, "but the Indians were *not* defeated in war, and do not consider themselves *subject* to any nation on earth. And if you will allow me to say so, unless they are treated with the utmost good faith and consideration, you will have trouble. They consider this river, especially above St. Ann's, their own. This is as true now as when the French occupied it. The reason they tolerated the French was because they made no claim of dominion over them, and they treated them as brothers. To be more brief, unless a like policy in now pursued by us, their subjection will only be consummated at a cost of more English lives and treasure than I like to contemplate."

Colonel Arbuthnot leaned forward, a thin smile about his lips. "I am curious to know, Mr. Cameron, how *you* would treat with them? The governor at Halifax, realizing that it is necessary, has done everything in his power to gain their goodwill. But if they start any trouble, I may find it expedient to send a few boat loads of soldiers up the river and burn their villages about their ears." He paused, and David said calmly:

"I will comment on your last statement first, Colonel Arbuthnot: They would ambush your soldiers, then retreat to attack again at a more favourable opportunity. Moreover, any injury done one tribe would be resented by every other from the Kennebec to Cape Sable, and you would find His Majesty's forces in Acadia involved in a conflict that would take a decade to win—if then.

"I would refer you, sir," he went on, "to Governor Cornwallis' desire, expressed to the home authorities, to wage a merciless war against the Indians of Acadia. I believe you know, sir, that for making the suggestion, he was twice reprimanded by the Lords of Trade, who suggested that gentler methods and offers of peace have more frequently prevailed with an Indian than the sword. Which brings me back to my reference to their priest being kept from them. And until he, or another, returns, it will be impossible for you to still their unrest. As I envision it, it is only a matter of a very short time until thousands of New England settlers come to the river, entirely changing existing conditions. But in the meantime, I would restrain any English colonials from going up the river farther than St. Ann's, above which, at Ek pa hawk, the Indians now have their most important village. As a matter of fact, Colonel Arbuthnot, I know the minds of the Indians, and that they will make war if their rights are infringed." He paused. Colonel Arbuthnot nodded and said:

"Naturally, a soldier resents advice from a civilian. However, Mr. Cameron, I must admit your reasoning is good, and I thank you."

David bowed to him, and taking another sip of wine, went on. "I shall now broach another matter, Colonel Arbuthnot, and since earlier you admitted that it has been a most grievous affair, and you did not enjoy seeing the sufferings of women and children, it gives me courage to say what I feel must be said." He paused a moment, then continued: "I refer to the manner in which these poor people have been treated in the past—treatment without precedent in modern warfare, and for which one can only find a parallel in medieval times in Europe. In short, sir, I refer to the late expulsion of these people from Nova Scotia as well as the indefensible slaughter and scalping by colonial soldiers that took place at St. Ann's two years ago. Also, sir, the transporting to Halifax of two hundred Acadians who came from Quebec following its capture. Pardon me, Colonel Arbuthnot, just a moment, please—"

For the commandant had risen, his face scarlet. "I will admit, sir, that you thought it was your duty as a guardian of His Majesty's peace in Acadia, but it was ill-advised, and—"

"You forget yourself, sir," cried Colonel Arbuthnot. "You are not in a position either to judge the act or its motive."

"Ah," said David, "but those Acadians had taken the oath of allegiance. They carried certificates to this effect from Judge Grahme, and permission from General Monckton to settle on the river. They came five hundred miles by river, lake, and portage, confident they would have justice accorded them. Instead, they were put on board ship and sent to that ill-advised politician, Governor Lawrence at Halifax."

Colonel Arbuthnot sank into his chair, his face pale.

"Mr. Cameron, as a matter of fact, when those people came to me, I was in a quandary what to do with them. I went to Halifax and consulted Governor Lawrence as to their disposition. He ordered me send them to him. In the circumstances, I could only comply." He paused, and David spoke:

"Colonel Arbuthnot, as a brother Scot, I am very happy that I have given you the opportunity to explain the situation. The blame then, rests on Governor Lawrence, and—"

"You have no right to blame the governor," interjected the colonel coldly. And added, "At any rate, Governor Lawrence died last autumn."

"I was not aware of that," said David. "But if he had lived a few years longer, he would have found that posterity would validate *my* judgment."

"Posterity be damned!" snapped Colonel Arbuthnot.

"No, no, posterity will not be damned," replied David. He rose quickly to his feet and stood before the irate colonel. He was barely conscious of the presence of his friend, Captain Fortesque. And standing there, he said:

"Colonel Arbuthnot, I have had the privilege of examining all the documents now reposing in the Archives in London that passed between the successive governors of Acadia and the Lords of Trade, as well as the Secretary of State, from the cession of Acadia in 1713 to the present time. And those documents conclusively show that the Acadians of Nova Scotia gave little cause for their banishment by Governor Lawrence. The home government again and again sent explicit orders to its representatives in Nova Scotia to deal leniently with the Acadians. Even at the very time that Governor Lawrence was executing the plan he had long entertained, orders were addressed to him condemning in energetic terms the project of banishment that he had submitted to the Lords of Trade. In other words, Lawrence, and his colonial advisers, intolerant descendants of the bigoted Puritans who settled New England, went over the heads of the Home Office and sent into exile these poor people whose—"

"They refused to take the oath of allegiance," interposed Colonel Arbuthnot.

"As submitted to them by Lawrence," parried David. "They had already taken a qualified oath during Governor Phillips' time; and it had his approval. They were ready to renew it under Lawrence, with the same qualifications exempting them from taking up arms."

"They were given the privilege of leaving the country," said Colonel Arbuthnot.

"That is quite correct, sir," said David. "In 1713, Queen Anne told them if they wished to leave within a year from the date of the treaty they would have the privilege of doing so, taking with them their movable effects, and the right to sell their immovable goods. But Nicholson, then governor, as well as some others following him, refused to let them depart."

"And, sir, what authority have you for this statement?" asked Colonel Arbuthnot.

The same as for all the other facts I have mentioned! From the Archives in London," answered David.

For a few moments the commandant made no comment. Indeed, he seemed at a loss for words. Finally he said stubbornly:

"A beaten enemy has no right to demand any such qualifying clause as insisted upon by the Acadians."

Said David, "Their demand for exemption was not without precedent. I refer, sir, to the acceptance of the Tsar of Russia to the settlement of the Mennonites in his Empire under the same condition of not bearing arms." He paused a moment, then went on:

"Colonel Arbuthnot, I came not here to quarrel. You were kind to me on my arrival, and gave me of your bread and wine. I am a plain-spoken man. Forgive me if I have incurred your displeasure. Frankly, I came here this afternoon to pay my respects to you, and to appeal to your sense of justice to deal leniently with any Acadians who remain on this river. I thank God that through my researches I have found proof that for all time exonerates the home government from blame in this lamentable affair—I mean the expulsion of these people.

"I have sat beside their firesides, and shared their humble fare. Those few who remain desire only to live in peace, to till their few acres, and worship in their own manner inherited from their forefathers. Surely, surely, sir, as victors, we can accord them these simple privileges. I ask you to imagine yourself in their place, and deal with them in future as you would be done by." Then he added, "Will ye not take my hand, man?" And he extended it.

For a few moments Arbuthnot spoke not. His face worked with conflicting emotions. Finally he said:

"My God, man, such a tongue ye have! But I have no doubt of your sincerity. If what you have told me about the home government is fact, it is the colonial administrators who have been to blame for what has happened. And yet…could I have acted differently about those two hundred Acadians? I do not know…I did what I conceived right at the moment." He paused, struck his forehead sharply with his open hand as if he would dash away all doubt, all vexations of spirit. Then, getting to his feet, he said, his voice gently sad:

"Gladly will I take your hand, Mr. Cameron. But remember, I am a soldier. I must obey my superiors so long as they command in this country. Yet, insofar as I am able, I will have as much consideration for your Acadians as lies in my power."

"That, my dear fellow countryman, is all I ask," said David. And he gave the Colonel's hand a grip that caused him to exclaim:

"What, mon! ye have travelled the road?"

"Aye," smiled David, "six, seven years ago. It has unlocked many doors for me all over the world."

As David and Captain Fortescue walked down to their waiting boat, the Captain said:

"Ah, David mon, I didna know ye could talk like that. It warmed the cockles of my heart. But times I was afraid ye would get nowhere. Aye, almost I expected him to say: 'Will it be swords, or pistols, Mr. Cameron?'"

David chuckled. "If he had, I would have said, 'Neither sir; but if ye must fight, I will fight ye with my own weapons.'"

"And pray, David, what would *they* be?" asked Captain Fortescue.

"Ah," answered David with another chuckle, "It would be my two fists, because I do not know the use of a sword, and I couldn't hit a barn door with a pistol. But, my friend, I am glad it did not go that far, because he is a kindly man, and I like him. The coming of the Acadians to Fort Frederick, so soon after the fall of Quebec, took him off balance. He was in a quandary; he felt unable to make a decision in their favour, after having received previous orders to deport any of them found on the river, and thought it advisable to consult the governor. We know the command that cold-blooded creature issued to him. As Arbuthnot said, the putting of it into effect was repugnant to his whole nature. I believe him."

That night David had a long talk with Tomah. Once more he begged the Chief to preserve peace with the English. He assured him their priest would be allowed to return. He said that Monsieur Chartier would come to the river the following spring. The ship bringing him would contain supplies for two truck houses he would establish on the river: one at the mouth of the Madocheka, the other possibly at Ek-pa-hawk above St. Ann's; and yet another on the Penobscot. Accompanying Monsieur Chartier would be a reliable Scot who had been in his employ for some years. He suggested that Tomah instruct his tribesmen to hold their furs until the arrival of the ship, which, being much smaller than the *Sheila Grahme*, would be able to navigate the river as far as St. Ann's.

Tomah was much pleased at this news. "My son is wise. My people will be happy." Then he added, "Will the ship bring sugar?"

"Yes," said David.

"And salt, my son?"

"Yes, my father."

"And mollylasses (molasses)?"

"Yes, there will be plenty."

"That is good," said Tomah.

In the morning Jeanne and David said farewell to the Chief. He was rowed to shore, and the boat returned to the ship.

The anchors were hoisted, the sails unfurled, and, for the wind was in the right quarter, they quickly filled. The ship began to move down the harbour.

David and Jeanne stood by the rail. They saw the tall figure of Tomah leaning on his gun, watching them. They waved to him. He raised one hand high above his head, then his voice drifted to them across the widening water.

"*Adio, Kuluwazu P'sazum.*"

It came clear and tuneful, like the notes of the bell in the chapel of his own Medowktek.

48

And so the good ship *Sheila Grahme* carried David Cameron and his Acadian bride down the harbour, and from thence along the coast to Passamaquoddy, where they found Monsieur Chartier awaiting them. And when they had taken him on board, the ship sailed out of the bay and across the leagues of sea to the port of Liverpool.

Here, after Jeanne had done some necessary shopping, David took her along the street to where, fourteen years before, he had found the printing establishment of Master Timothy Cole and Job Dawkings, who had printed his little pamphlet describing his adventures in America. But to his disappointment the Sign of the Glove was no longer over the door, and he was informed by the present tenant of the place, who dealt in fish, that Timothy Cole was no longer living, and Mr. Dawkings was now making his home with a daughter in Kent.

The following day, David, his bride, and Monsieur Chartier took post to London, where they found rooms at The Lion Inn.

The next afternoon, having sought and been granted an interview with Mr. William Pitt, he went to the great prime minister's room at the appointed hour, and was ushered inside by a footman. Mr. Pitt was seated at his desk writing, but rose, smiled, and offered David his hand. When he was seated the Prime Minister courteously informed him that, due to pressure of State business, he would only be able to allow him fifteen minutes of his time. David thanked him, but added that what he had to say was also a very serious matter of state, for it concerned the Acadian people in His Majesty's colony of Nova Scotia, most of whom had been ruthlessly torn from their homes and sent into exile, against the expressed wishes of His

Majesty's Government, while the remainder were at present hiding in remote places, their lot no better than that of the Indians.

Now, with raised eyebrows, the Prime Minister said, "You speak with assurance, Mr. Cameron. But first I would like to know what authority you have for your last statement; secondly, how you came by the information—not generally known—that His Majesty's Government was not responsible for the deportation of these people?"

Then David said, "As for the first part of your question, Mr. Pitt:—I returned but two days ago from the Saint John River, once included in the ancient boundaries of Acadia, where I had opportunity to get first-hand information about the condition of the refugees. For the rest:—two years ago I was privileged to examine in the archives here, all those documents that passed between the successive governors of Nova Scotia and the Lords of Trade, from the cession of Acadia to His Majesty's Government up to the time of the expulsion."

"Ah," said Mr. Pitt, "and may I ask, Mr. Cameron, how it was that you were accorded this rather unusual privilege?"

"That is easily answered, sir," said David. "I carried letters of introduction from my cousins, the Honourable Simon Fraser, and the Reverend Robert MacPherson, to the Secretary of the Lords of Trade. It seems," he ended with a smile, "that these were the means of opening the doors of the Archives to me."

At which Mr. Pitt, looking much surprised, said, "You are cousin to the Honourable Simon Fraser, the commander of Fraser's Highlanders, and of the Reverend Robert MacPherson?"

"Yes, sir," answered David.

There is a legend in the Highlands, which David would neither confirm or deny, that at this the Honourable Mr. Pitt got quickly to his feet, and reaching out his hand again seized David's, and wringing it heartily, said:

"Mr. Cameron, when you mentioned that your coming had to do with the lot of the Acadian people, I at once made up my mind to extend the fifteen minute interview for as long as you found necessary. The fact that you are a relative of the Honourable Simon Fraser, and of the chaplain of his regiment, Reverend Robert

MacPherson, makes your visit today all the more acceptable. Please to go on."

"I thank you, Mr. Pitt," said David. Then with a smile: "The Reverend Robert MacPherson is lovingly known in the Highlands as Caipal More, because of his great size."

"Ah," said Mr. Pitt, "a man I should much like to meet. I have heard that at the Battle of the Plains, while ministering to a wounded comrade, and being attacked by two Indians, he took each of them by the scruff of the neck, rattled their pates together, then flung them far from him. Ah, yes, a man I would much like to know. Please continue, Mr. Cameron."

So the talk went on for two whole hours; the result of which all the English speaking world knows. For the Prime Minister there and then assured David that the Acadian who had been deported, as well as those who had escaped and were in hiding, would be allowed to return and once more take up peaceful domicile in their homeland. But however sincere the expressed intention of Mr. Pitt, not until four or five years had passed was it possible to put it into effect; and in the meantime, despite the protests of the Secretary of State, Governor Belcher, who succeeded Lawrence, and his successor, Wilmott, were responsible for further deportations.

But following David's conference with the Prime Minister, a law was passed, giving any of His Majesty's subjects the right to engage in the fur trade in Acadia (or Nova Scotia, as it was now officially called).

Before David left, the great Pitt again shook his hand. And David said, his heart beating with happiness, "I thank you, sir, for your humane consideration of the whole problem." To which Mr. Pitt replied:

"For some time I have had it under consideration to right a great wrong. Your coming to-day will be an impetus to its early fulfilment."

Light-footed and light-hearted, David Cameron departed from the great man, and proceeded to the inn where he had left Jeanne and Monsieur Chartier. There he told them the result of his mission. And when he had done, Jeanne threw her arms about his neck, and wept a little, as women do in moments of great joy, and told him she had known all along that he would attain what he set out to accomplish.

Following a few more days in London, where Jeanne made many purchases dear to a woman's heart, David, his wife, and Monsieur Chartier returned to Liverpool, boarded the *Sheila Grahme*, and sailed up the coast to Scotland.

And so, in the Royal Burgh of Aberdeen, she who had been Jeanne Chartier took up her new life in the old house in the Broad Gate, that for generations had belonged to David's forbears. And she often said to her husband in later years:

"It was as though I had been away a long time, and had returned home."

THE END

Woodstock, New Brunswick
(Formerly known as Acadia)
1952

EDITOR'S AFTERWORD

George Frederick Clarke started writing *David Cameron's Return* in 1949. He had written no fiction since 1936, when he wrote a book that he called *Tomah the Maliseet Chief*. But after three or four book rejections in the early 30s, he was discouraged. He put that manuscript aside and wrote nothing for the next twelve years but a monograph on his archaeological work. Then in 1948 he was spurred into revising *Tomah*; by the end of the year it had a publisher, and a new name: *David Cameron's Adventures*.

GFC badly wanted to get back to writing fiction—but could he, after being blocked for so long? Revising a book was, after all, a lot easier than writing one from scratch.

He needn't have worried. When he started a sequel to *David Cameron* in 1950, it fairly flowed onto the page. That summer, on a fishing trip, he met the publisher of the newly founded Brunswick Press, who asked if he would let the Press see the new book. GFC sent them *The Wooing of Mademoiselle Chartier* in early 1951, and they took it—but not under that title. GFC consented to changing it, but under protest; in this courteous business letter from its editor at the Press there is an undertone of despair.

> As to the title we still feel that it should be changed, but so far we have not thought of a better one. It is the oldfashioned expression "The wooing" which worries us most. What would you think of "The Rival Lords of Acadia" or "Borders of New France"?[1]

---

1   Brunswick Press, Blair Gilmour, ed. Letter to G.F. Clarke, 2 February 1952. George Frederick Clarke Fonds, MG L 47. Unprocessed. Archives & Special Collections, University of New Brunswick Libraries. Fredericton, New Brunswick

In the end they agreed on the anodyne *Return to Acadia*. There was a plan to have a French edition, but it came to nothing.

Return to Acadia / David Cameron's Return was the last novel GFC wrote.

The sources of the story

David Cameron's Return unfolds against a large backdrop: a long, world-wide, almost continuous series of wars between France and England that lasted from about 1689 to 1815, a series that is sometimes called the "Second Hundred Years' War." David was kidnapped near the beginning of one episode in this conflict, King George's War (1744–1748). The Expulsion of the Acadians took place during the Seven Years' War (1754-1763).

GFC had read extensively in the history of the period,[2] his facts are probably correct, though his interpretation of the British government's involvement in the Expulsion may well be open to question. I am not a historian, but I suspect that the British government's hands were not so clean as GFC wanted to believe. He was an old-fashioned romantic patriot, with a profound allegiance to "the mother country," and as unwilling to believe wrong of England as if she had indeed been his mother. Yet by temperament he was always passionately engaged on the side of victims of injustice: that engagement breathes throughout this book. I think he reconciled the monumental injustice done to the Acadians with his belief in British disinterested idealism by convincing himself that Governor Lawrence and the New Englanders had acted on their own, without orders from England.

---

2   His primary sources include Marc Lescarbot and Nicolas Denys. If his history of Acadia (1958) is any guide, his reading in secondary sources was limited to historians who wrote in late nineteenth century, such as Beamish Murdoch, Francis Parkman, James Hannay, W.F. Ganong and J.C. Webster. But few modern histories of the region existed in the mid-twentieth century, when GFC was doing research for this book; or for his own history of Acadia, *Too Small a World: the Story of Acadia* (1958) and his pamphlet, *The True Story of the Expulsion of the Acadians* (1955), which makes the same case for British innocence of ethnic cleansing that David puts to Colonel Arbuthnot in this book.

Interested readers can judge for themselves. There are good articles in Wikipedia about the historical events and persons in this book; and references to numerous modern books about the history of Acadia.

GFC and Robert Louis Stevenson had at least two things in common. Both could write an exciting adventure story: *David Cameron's Adventures;* Stevenson's *Kidnapped.* And neither of them could write convincingly about love between men and women. RLS wrote a sequel to *Kidnapped,* in which its hero woos and wins the lovely Catriona after many difficulties. *Kidnapped* was an international best-seller. *Catriona* was not. *David Cameron's Return* actually sold better than *David Cameron's Adventures* (for reasons, see below), but not because of its heroine. Jeanne Chartier is less a woman than an engraving of Evangeline, with "a pure oval face," a voice "like a lilting brook," a "calm and spiritual beauty."

The most vivid character in the story is Tomah, and perhaps the most vivid scene is the one when David lies close to death and Tomah uses his *me-ta-o-lin* powers to cure him. He frightens Jeanne and shocks the priest, but GFC is neither shocked nor frightened. He is interested. Unlike them, he is not in thrall to the idea that any religion—in particular Christianity—is better than any other. Tomah's rite is like Jeanne's telling her beads or praying to St. Ann: an expression of a universal impulse to prayer. GFC does not see it as an act of primitive superstition; nor, conversely, does he describe it with any New-Ageish deference, *avant la lettre*, to the superior wisdom of simpler ways of life. He knew better. He would have described a Catholic mass or a Hindu puja in the same spirit, had he had occasion to.

Reception

David Cameron's Return/Return to Acadia sold much better than *David Cameron's Adventures*—chiefly, I believe, because *Adventures* was published in Scotland and marketed in Canada (its natural market) by the Ryerson Press, who were lackadaisical about stocking it and sending it out to bookstores, and hardly bothered to publicise it. The Brunswick Press, in contrast, gave *Return* a decent amount of publicity—and kept good track of stock and orders.

The book was published in both hardcover and paperback, the only one of GFC's books to appear in a softcover edition in his lifetime. Curiously, the hardcover consistently outsold the paperback by about a third. The book had substantial sales for many years. For instance:

Year	Copies Sold
1958	685
1960	1843
1961	1854

By 1964, however, it was selling less than 200 a year, and from 1968 onwards the sales dropped to nothing. But it had had a long run.[3]

It received far more reviews than *David Cameron's Adventures* had had, probably because the Brunswick Press promoted it properly; and they were mostly favourable. *Maclean's Magazine* called it "a moving story of romance and adventure." The *Ottawa Evening Journal* said:

> [GFC] is a student of ancient Canadian folk-lore and brings to his task an authority and unusual zest The majesty of the primeval background as well as his creation of Tomah— unquestionably one of the immortals in literature—reveal the author's genius for descriptive writing as well as his ability to bring his people to life.

Its Acadian background earned it a review in the *Louisiana Traveler*,[4] and at least two reviews in Acadian papers. One of them called GFC:

---

3 These figures come from royalty statements. Some of these statements were destroyed in an attic fire after GFC's death; I have none for the years 1952-1957.

4 Many Acadians were deported to Louisiana, where their descendants, the Cajuns, have a culture with close affinities to that of eighteenth-century Acadia.

non seulement un historien averti et au courant de notre
histoire, mais, et peut-être à cause de cela, un sincère ami du
peuple acadien qui ne craint pas de condamner, à l'occasion et
en termes non équivoques, la déportation de 1755.[5]

The text, and the word "Indians"

I have worked from the first edition of *Return to Acadia*, silently
correcting a few typos and inconsistencies. I have also removed a
few proper names of historical personages who are mentioned once,
but play no part whatever in the story.

GFC lived before the term "First Nations" was in common use.
He called First Nations peoples Indians, and it was what they then
called themselves. I have not changed his usage, or his spellings of
the names of First Nations peoples.

The cover and map

The cover of the first edition of *David Cameron's Return/Return
to Acadia* was a dull grayscale photo of a bit of birchbark. For this
edition I have used an illustration from *David Cameron's Adventures*,
of a scene which occurs in both books: the moment when David
and Tomah meet again after fourteen years. The original drawing,
by Will Nickless, was in grayscale (and still is, in the new edition
of *David Cameron's Adventures*). For the cover of this book I have
coloured it.

The map of Acadia was printed on the endpapers of *Return to
Acadia*. I have digitally restored it.

About myself

I am the daughter of GFC's elder daughter, Jane; GFC was my
grandfather. In 2015 Chapel Street Editions published *The Last
Romantic*, my story of his life.

---

5   "Un Livre Récent sur l'Acadie." Rev. of *Return to Acadia.*
    Unknown Newspaper (n.d. [1953]). George Frederick Clarke
    Fonds, MG L 47. Unprocessed. Archives & Special Collections,
    University of New Brunswick Libraries. Fredericton, New
    Brunswick

Chapel Street Editions has undertaken a grand publishing project called the George Frederick Clarke Project, to publish all of GFC's books. I am editing the series. Eight books of the GFC Project are now in print:

> My biography of GFC: *The Last Romantic: The Life George Frederick Clarke, Master Storyteller of New Brunswick* (2015)

And the following books by GFC:

> *Six Salmon Rivers—and Another*, his first fishing memoir (2015)

> *The Ghost of Nackawick Portage: the Collected Short Stories of George Frederick Clarke*, the first collection of all his surviving short stories (2015)

> *The Song of the Reel*, his second fishing memoir (2016)

> *Jimmy-Why and Noël Polchies: their Adventures in the Great Woods*, his two books for young children, complete in one volume (2016)

> *Someone Before Us: Buried History in Central New Brunswick*, his memoir of his archaeological finds and adventures (2016)

> *David Cameron's Adventures* (2018)

> *David Cameron's Return* (2018), the sequel to *David Cameron's Adventures*, originally published under the title *Return to Acadia*.

The next two books in the project are *Chris in Canada*, the story of an English boy who emigrates with his family to a farm on Howland Ridge, in New Brunswick, overlooking Taffa Lake; and *Chris in the Wilderness*, in which Chris and Noel Polchies go into the woods in winter. *Chris in the Wilderness* was never published, but it is one of GFC's best books.

Acknowledgment

As always, and for many very good reasons, I want to thank my publishers, Keith, Brendan and Ellen Helmuth, of Chapel Street Editions.

Mary Bernard
Cambridge, England,
January 2018

PUBLISHER'S AFTERWORD

The Imagination of George Frederick Clarke and the Gift of Storytelling

When *David Cameron's Return* (*Return to Acadia*) was first published in 1952, it carried the subtitle, *A Historical Romance.* By this time in the development of modern literature, the category of romance was no longer used for serious writing. Romance was out-of-date at best and trivial at worst. Critics whose professional standing depended on being up-to-date with modern critical trends looked down on historical novels and paid them scant attention unless they were by authors with established literary reputations.

Fortunately for New Brunswick and for all lovers of great storytelling, George Frederick Clarke paid no attention to the gatekeepers of modern literature. He was not interested in keeping up with the changing fashions of literary expression. In writing his short stories* and in the David Cameron novels, he was interested in telling stories that gripped his imagination and provided readers with a vivid historical sense of people, place, and circumstance.

Clarke was deeply interested in the human stories of his home region.

David Cameron's Adventures sets the stage and *David Cameron's Return* thrusts the reader deeply into the layered cultural history of the Wolastoqiyik homeland – the land that came to be called Acadia, then Nova Scotia, and eventually New Brunswick.

---

*　*The Ghost of Nackawick Portage: The Collected Short Stories of George Frederick Clarke.* Edited by Mary Bernard. Chapel Street Editions, Woodstock, New Brunswick, 2015.

The fact that *David Cameron's Return* is structured by a romantic quest, does not detract from Clarke's vivid portrayal of the region's history and of the cultural, economic, and political life of the time. In addition, his heartfelt descriptions of the rivers, forests, and landscapes that form the predominant environment of the book are a tantalizing forecast of what is to come when he later writes his classic books about fishing and the fishing life on New Brunswick's storied rivers.[*]

We can be thankful that George Frederick Clarke stayed true to the gift of storytelling that was his forte. His books are anchored in a sense of place and continue to be of interest to readers who value this anchoring. The David Cameron books, in particular, combine history and geography in a way that can be followed closely on maps of the terrain. And, if readers are so inclined, they can visit the very sites along the Wolastoq that are described in *David Cameron's Return*. Opening up this engagement with history in an imaginative and reflective way is the storytelling gift Clarke brought to his writing.

Historical romances were certainly old hat by the 1950s, but literary gatekeepers who make such determinations fail to reckon with the fact that the unfolding of the human story and its expression in literature is not a linear phenomenon in which new forms cancel out older forms. Storytelling in many forms continues to populate the branches of the great tree of literature. It's not a matter of asking whether this or that form of storytelling any longer has a vital place in human cultural expression, but rather whether of the expression of the form is well done, whether the characters stick in the mind of the reader and whether the window of imagination the writer has opened is ample to a fully rounded sense of the human condition.

Although I had previously read George Frederick Clarke's later books, including his archaeological memoir,[*] I had not read *David Cameron's Adventures* or *David Cameron's Return* until preparing to

---

[*] *Six Salmon Rivers and Another*, 4th edition. Edited by Mary Bernard. Chapel Street Editions; Woodstock, New Brunswick, 2015. *Song of the Reel*, 2nd edition. Edited by Mary Bernard. Chapel Street Editions; Woodstock New Brunswick, 2016.

[*] *Someone Before Us: Buried History in Central New Brunswick*, 4th edition. Edited by Mary Bernard. Chapel Street Editions, Woodstock, New Brunswick, 2016.

publish new editions. I knew they were historical novels written in a pre-modern style, but pre-modern is not a pejorative term for me. I was swept up in Clarke's telling of these stories in much the same way I was affected, many years ago as a young reader, by the early stories of Zane Grey about the colonial settler's invasion of the Ohio River Valley and the defense of their homeland mounted by the region's Indigenous Peoples.

As a novelist, Clarke may be pre-modern in style, but as a storyteller and as creator of characters that stick in the imagination long after the covers have been closed, his books rank high in timeless durability for those who love historical fiction and who raise a cheer when a heartfelt romance overcomes all barriers and carries the day. It would be a pinched view of literary achievement that does not include the amplitude of such storytelling.

Keith Helmuth
Chapel Street Editions
Woodstock, New Brunswick

Glossary of Place Names, Old Words, Distances

*Place names are marked in the text with the symbol * at first occurrence. Old words are marked with $*

Place names

Maliseet name	*modern English name*
Ah-jem-sec river	Jemseg river
Chic-seen-i-beg falls	Grand Falls
Ek-pa-hawk	Silverwood (just below the mouth of the Keswick)
Et-la-guim-ek river	Becaguimec river
Great Sa-gûm-o mountain	Mount Carleton
Lustook river	Aroostook river
Mamozekel river	still so named
Na-goot river	Tobique river, after a Maliseet chief, Noel Toubic or Tobec (1706-1767), who lived at the river's mouth. (William Baillie Hamilton, *Place Names of Atlantic Canada*.)
Na-goot-sis river	Little Tobique river
Nalaisk river	Serpentine river
Pulam river	Salmon river
St. Ann's	Fredericton

Old words

bastion . . . . part of the defensive wall of a fortification, projecting out from the encircling curtain wall, so that the defenders can fire in several directions.

cariole . . . . in Canada, an open sledge with seating for one or more people.

fosse . . . . . a defensive ditch.

league. . . . . 4.8 km, see table below.

lucivee . . . . the Maliseet name for Canada lynx.

overhaul . . . to catch up with.
peltries . . . . animal pelts, especially undressed skins.
sagûm . . . . . chief, cf. "sachem".
senna tea . . . a laxative.
truck house . . a storehouse for goods used for or received in
               barter, especially in the colonial period.
               —https://www.merriam-webster.com

Distances given in leagues in the book, with modern equivalents

Leagues	Miles	Kilometres
1	3	4.8
3	9	14.5
5	15	24
12	36	58
18	54	87
30	90	145
50	150	240
90	270	435